March Forth

Dedicated to all who read it,
And especially to my beautiful niece, Alexandra; may you follow your
artistic pursuits as far as they will take you.

<u>Prologue</u>

The man sat on a bed in a run-down motel room, whispering over and over, "This is a bed. I am sitting on a bed. It is a bed. This is a bed." He was desperately trying to remember; it was an insignificant thing, but he just wanted to remember something. Anything.

The thing with the numbers on it started making a noise; he jumped a bit, and then stared at it, willing it to stop. It did. He turned his attention back to the task at hand, which had been....

It had been....

He was trying to remember something. What was it? He knew it, he knew he knew it; he just had to think....

Then he was sitting on a beach, watching the sunset over the ocean. He blinked. This isn't where he was before. He had been sitting on the... on the thing, and the thing that made the noise... did the thing. Right? He hadn't been here.

A deep voice behind him said, "You don't even realize what's happening, do you, David?"

David. That sounded familiar. Something clicked in his brain, and he turned to look at the speaker as he asked, "I'm David?"

The speaker, a tall man in flowing robes, gave him a wan smile that did not reach his sad, pitying eyes. "Yes, you are David. Try to remember that. Try to remember all that you know; when you do, you'll be able to fix this."

David stared at the tall man, wide-eyed, wondering what he was talking about. "What do I know?"

The robed man made a sound somewhere between a laugh and a sob, and shook his head slowly. He stared at the ocean for several long seconds before replying. "You know very little, right now. But you did know many things. You knew the cause and solution to the problem you're having now. You knew what was important in life. You knew me. You knew you weren't alone."

"Wow," David said, nonplussed. He certainly had known a lot, it seemed.

The robed man continued staring out at the vast ocean, his gaze on the distant horizon. He appeared to be deep in thought. After a few moments, he said, "What is important to you right now, David?"

David's face screwed up from the effort of concentrating. After several long moments full of deep thought, he looked up at the robed man and stammered, "I...I'm David?"

"Telling," the robed man murmured, mostly to himself. He heaved a sigh and said, "David, my friend, I need you to hear me right now, and remember my words. Can you do that?"

David shrugged, having no idea whether he could.

"You must use your gifts. You must find a world where you can be safe, and you must find me again. Do you understand me?"

David stared blankly at him, showing no sign whatsoever of understanding, so the robed man repeated, "Use your gifts. Find a world where you can be safe. Find me again. Say it."

"Use gifts. Find....um...."

"Find a world where you can be safe."

"Find a world where I can be safe."

"Find me again."

"Find me again."

"No, you have to find me again."

"Find you again."

The robed man nodded, satisfied. "I want you to repeat those to yourself, all the time. Concentrate on those instructions more than anything else."

David nodded, and took up the new chant. "Use my gifts. Find a world where I can be safe. Find you again. Use my gifts. Find a world where I can be safe. Find you again."

The robed man placed a hand on his head, willing the words to stay in his mind. When he took his hand away, David blinked in the bright sunlight and looked around, confused. He was alone again, huddled on a sidewalk in the cold. People bustled past, but no one noticed him. He had no idea where he was, or how he had gotten there, or where the robed man had gone. He felt like he should have control over such things, and that maybe he once had, but he wasn't sure if that was even true. With no one and nothing to verify the feeling, it might be safe to assume he had always been tossed about like this, from place to place, with no control. He wished he knew for sure.

Desperate for something to focus on, he resumed his chant.

"Use my gifts. Find a world where I can be safe. Find you again."

He repeated the words until they lost all meaning. He repeated them until he forgot how to say the words, and he kept trying to repeat them even when the syllables he uttered had no resemblance to the original words. It didn't matter. He could repeat the idea. He took comfort in the fact that these words came from somewhere outside of

4

himself, from something other than the all-encompassing sense of loss and confusion that had become his life.

He kept up his chant for nearly two decades, as he aimlessly wandered through space and time. He often couldn't remember what the words really meant, but they somehow made him feel better.

Deanna

It was late February, but the temperature had unexpectedly risen to forty degrees for just one, glorious day. All of the majestic icicles and dazzling, naturally-formed ice sculptures that had been developing over the long, unusually bitter winter months were starting to melt and drip down to non-existence. As a result, parts of Main Street in Woodford had become tiny rivers; alleys became tributaries; parking lots served as the lakes into which they all poured. It was a welcome sight to most of the town's residents, as it signified the imminent arrival of long awaited spring. However, the weather reports were all calling for eight inches of snow that night, which caused a lot of moaning throughout the little New Jersey town (and the entire Eastern Seaboard, for that matter) about how it seemed they would never see grass or blooming trees again.

Despite the grey skies and general dampness in the air, Deanna decided to take advantage of the briefly milder temperature and run some errands, starting with a trip to the laundromat. She lived right in the heart of downtown Woodford, a bustling little town that had recently developed aspirations toward becoming a cultural destination. The presence of a train station which could bring residents into New York City had led to the development of new luxury apartment buildings and the influx of various restaurants, shops, and the like. The powers that be were trying to attract young, urban professionals to move into the town and commute to work in the (comparably overpriced) city. It was a risky move, and many of the luxury apartments still stood empty. However, all of the new development made life that much more convenient for Deanna. The laundromat, like the grocery store and basically any other amenities she may need or want, stood within a few blocks of her apartment. She grabbed her laundry bag and walked down Main Street, humming while she walked. For the first time in a long time, she was in a good mood.

The winter had, indeed, been a long, hard one for Deanna, in more ways than just enduring the sub-freezing temperatures. She had left her job at the BitterSweet Bistro the previous fall for, as she had explained to people, "personal reasons." In short, she had had a bit of a breakdown. There had been external reasons for it – never-ending money problems, the emotional backlash she was experiencing from the latest guy in the long line of bad choices that had been her love life, and so on – but what it boiled down to was, she had a breakdown. She had been feeling bad about herself and, thanks to anxiety-induced insomnia, not

6

sleeping enough. She started drinking heavily, which is widely acknowledged as a time honored problem solving strategy which really helps by making everything much, much worse, so the original problems seem small in comparison. She lashed out at the owner of the BitterSweet, unleashing every negative thought she had ever had about him, his business, and his employees. She gave her two weeks' notice, and he told her to take a few days off to think about it. That made her even angrier, as it felt like he had taken her power away. She felt like it was her choice to throw away her job and generally freak out, and damn it, she was going to do it. She never went back.

After leaving the BitterSweet, she floundered from one dissatisfying, temporary restaurant job to another. She could not find "the right job," one where she made enough money to pay her bills but could also hold on to whatever shreds of sanity she had. Corporate chains, with their homogenized scripts and unending rules, made her feel like her soul was sucked out by the time clock on which she punched in; conversely, in privately owned restaurants, she had no recourse to take if employees were being treated unfairly (like the one little café where her boss would regularly hit on her, then give her a small section – therefore reducing her income for the night – when she didn't respond positively). Her already-dire financial situation plummeted even further downhill. She was thirty seven years old, and had had to borrow money from her parents to avoid being evicted from her apartment. It was humiliating. Deanna was beginning to think her entire life had been a waste, but she rallied as well as she could. She filled out job applications every day, and repeated affirmations in the mirror to convince herself that she was worthy of a good job. She signed up for free webinars that claimed they would help fix her "money mindset" and make her a more successful person. She meditated daily, focusing on manifesting "the right job." Still, nothing changed.

Just recently, Deanna had decided she needed to get out of the restaurant industry. She felt like her current situation might be the universe's way of telling her it was time for a change. Though she'd been serving and bartending for years, the unpredictable nature of the business was getting to her. Her income was based solely on tips, and it was almost impossible to accurately predict how much she would make in any given week. Her attempts to work out a budget for herself never seemed to work out, as she seemed unable to estimate her baseline income and often overestimated what it would be. She needed something more stable, more dependable. Leaving the industry was not something that she had even thought of for over a decade; working in restaurants was just what she did. The decision to change careers had felt like an epiphany.

She wasn't sure what she was going to do – she wasn't sure what else she *could* do, because she had been in the industry for so long – but even making the decision felt good. It just felt right. She hoped, as she had hoped so many times before, that this might be the decision that would lead to her finally getting her life together.

She had been working on a new resume for a couple of days, and finally got it finished just that morning. She had even sent a few copies out to receptionist jobs she saw advertised online. She was feeling unusually good about herself, and the relatively nice weather only improved her mood.

"No matter how long, dark, and cold winter is, spring will eventually come," she thought.

As she walked toward the laundromat, she hummed along to the music that played from hidden speakers on the lampposts that lined Main Street – at the moment, it was Bob Marley's song "Three Little Birds" - and she truly hoped that every little thing was gonna be alright.

Woodford's Main Street was fairly crowded with people from all walks of life, enjoying the momentary respite from the harsh winter. Mothers pushed babies in carriages; lawyers and their clients, wearing suits, strolled from the court house to their favorite eateries while intently discussing their cases; joggers weaved around all of them, determined not to let the leisurely pace of pedestrians slow down their heart rate. Here and there, the homeless people of Woodford sat on benches or leaned against storefronts, watching everyone go by.

Although it was a small, rather quaint town, Woodford had more than a few homeless people and "interesting" characters. It was the county seat, after all, and therefore home to the county welfare office, jail, and various other institutions that attracted what some called "the undesirable element." Deanna never minded them. She had always believed in treating everyone, no matter what their station in life, with kindness and respect. It may have been her Irish Catholic upbringing, or it may have been all of the fairy tales she read as a child in which old beggar women turned into witches or fairies and repaid kindness with treasure, or punished rudeness with hexes. Whatever the reason, it was simply Deanna's nature to be nice to everyone.

Because of that innate sense of politeness, she paused and smiled when she turned into the walkway leading off Main Street and a robed man boomed, "Good day, my queen!" Many people would not have done so. The man was about six and a half feet tall, with dark skin and dreadlocks that fell to just below his shoulders. He appeared to be wearing brightly colored, flowing robes; upon closer inspection, Deanna realized they were made from old bedsheets. Though the day was the warmest it had been in a while, it was still far too chilly for him to be wearing the sandals that he wore. He held, in his left hand, some kind of a staff made from a fallen tree branch, which he pounded on the ground for emphasis when he greeted her.

"And to you," she responded politely, with a smile and nod.

"You honor me," the man bellowed, his voice echoing. The walkway was a lovely little spot, with brick underfoot and wooden trellises overhead, between two brick buildings. It provided the perfect acoustics for his rich, deep voice, making his words seem even more theatrical than they were.

They were alone in the walkway, and he was standing directly in her path, so she said, "If you'll pardon me, sir, I need to get to the laundromat."

"I would not dare to block you from your chosen path, my lady," he said as he stood to the side with a sweeping gesture, bidding her to pass.

"Thank you," she said, a bit awkwardly. "Have a wonderful day."

"You as well, my lady! May it be filled with love and light! Be gentle with yourself!"

Deanna, carrying her laundry bag over her shoulder, turned to smile at him, and saw that he was gazing at her with a fond look on his face. "What an odd character," she thought; nevertheless, something about his totally irrational and inexplicably worshipful attitude toward her made her feel good about herself, somehow.

Although Woodford had its share of homelessness, most of the usual cast of characters was well known around town. There was, for example, "The Piano Man," who never spoke to or even looked at anyone, but would occasionally stop in the middle of the sidewalk, eyes closed, and wiggle his fingers in the air, looking for all the world as if he were playing a grand piano that no one else could see. There were times Deanna imagined she could almost hear the music.

Then there was "The Friendly Gargoyle," a poor soul with bug eyes and a distorted smile who would squat on benches, waving and smiling at anyone who passed by. He bore more than a passing resemblance to one of the gargoyle statues that sat atop one of the town's churches, but his seemingly eternal state of good cheer made him a welcome sight for most of the town. Thus, he earned his nickname.

Then, of course, there was the inimitable "Rasta Man," though Deanna hadn't seen him in months; she hoped his absence meant he had found someplace warm to shelter his frail form during the harsh winter. He had been an unforgettable character, with a single, waist length black dreadlock shot through with grey streaks, and dark, haunted eyes that looked as if he had come from the depths of hell. He walked around town, talking to himself loudly in strange, unintelligible syllables, as if he had forgotten how to use language but still had a lot to say. He had earned the name "The Rasta Man" only because of the dreadlock; his other features were too off-putting to be used as a nickname.

There were many others, too, who had hung around Woodford for years and were recognizable to all. The robed man, though, was someone Deanna had never seen before. She definitely would have remembered even a passing encounter; he was not someone you could easily forget.

As she reached the laundromat and loaded her clothes into the washer, Deanna vaguely wondered if the Rasta Man and the robed man knew each other. They both had dreads, after all. She smiled to herself, remembering her last attempt at conversation with the Rasta Man, the previous August.

He had been a fixture around town that summer, when she was still working at the BitterSweet Bistro. Sometimes, he would see her smoking a cigarette while she walked to work, and through a series of incomprehensible syllables and frantic gestures, he would ask her to give him a cigarette. She always gave him one.

Though he was a small, malnourished-looking man, the Rasta Man was a little scary. It was his eyes. There was an otherworldly, haunted expression in his eyes that made him look like some kind of an alien, a refugee from another dimension where life had not treated him well. The fact that no one could understand what he said, and his habit of talking to himself, did not help matters. Most everyone gave the Rasta Man a wide berth when they saw him coming, including Deanna, at first. After he bummed a cigarette off her once or twice, though, she decided he was harmless, though his eyes always made her feel a little uncomfortable. She mostly just felt bad for him, despite being slightly afraid of him.

A few times, he drifted in the front door of the BitterSweet Bistro like a leaf on the wind, and just stood there looking around at the walls like he didn't know where he was. Usually, this happened early in the day while she was opening the bar, before customers came in. She would hold out a cigarette, knowing that's what he was looking for, and he would take it from her and leave again without a word.

The last time the Rasta Man came in, she heard him before she saw him. They were closed for a private party that day, and she and her coworkers were bustling around, moving tables and bringing out the chafing dishes for the buffet. She heard her coworker Drew talking by the front door, telling someone they couldn't come in because the restaurant was closed. Then the unmistakable voice of the Rasta Man sounded, shouting something that sounded like, "Lack hanna leeb nice ladyyy, jab!"

She had gone to the front, pushing the irate-but-intimidated Drew to the side gently and holding up a cigarette. The Rasta Man took it and inclined his head toward the door slightly, as if inviting her outside, so she followed him. It was so rare that any of his attempts at communication made sense, she didn't see how she could turn down the subtle invitation.

While they were outside, smoking cigarettes together, he talked more than she had ever heard him talk before. Most of it was obscure gibberish that she couldn't understand. Even those words that she could actually decipher made no sense, like when he said, "Had a new motorcycle, brand new, dunno where I left it. Maybe Ohio?" Despite her lack of comprehension, she smiled and nodded as if chatting with an old friend; she felt like he needed someone to talk to. Finally Rasta Man looked her dead in the eye, with those sad, scared, haunted, crazy eyes of his, and said, as clearly as he could, "Is it safe to be here, Lady?"

"Of course," she said. "Have a good day."

He looked up at the sky and then just wandered away, looking around him with an air of fascinated confusion that made Deanna think of a newborn child.

Remembering that day now, she smiled, picturing him riding a brand new motorcycle down a highway in California or someplace similarly warm and wonderful. Although she knew it was highly unlikely, if not impossible, that he had ever owned a brand new motorcycle, much less lost and found one, it was what she hoped had happened to him. She wanted to believe that wherever he was, he was happy, healthy, and well –fed, and had found his brand new motorcycle.

"God knows I've made some bad life choices," she thought. "If it weren't for my parents bailing me out, I could easily have become one of the homeless of Woodford."

She shook her head, trying to clear it of those familiar but unwelcome self-deprecating thoughts, and looked at the clock on the

11

wall. She decided to head to the coffee shop down the street while her clothes were in the washing machine; hanging around in the laundromat was just depressing.

As she opened the door of the coffee shop, a merry little bell jingled to announce her presence. It was a cozy place, with couches and armchairs set up around little tables, and books and magazines laid out for patrons to enjoy while they sipped their coffee or enjoyed their snacks.

"Oh, hey, Deanna!" Paul, the owner, exclaimed as he emerged from behind a curtain that separated the little kitchen from the front of the store. "Haven't seen you in a while, how've you been?"

"I'm well. Same old, same old."

"How's the job hunt going?"

"Nothing yet," she admitted. "Just revamped my resume, though. Thinking about getting out of the restaurant industry."

"Oh, yeah? I don't blame you, it's a tough business," Paul replied. His eyes, Deanna noticed, looked a little glazed, and he smelled like he had just emerged from the inside of a bong. Paul was a sweet guy who had never quite mentally left the 1960's. "Good luck with everything."

"Thanks, Paul," she replied, and he disappeared behind the curtain again without asking if she wanted anything.

After standing awkwardly for a few seconds, she called, "Hey, Paul?"

His head appeared around the curtain. "Oh, hey, Deanna. What's up?"

"Could I... if you're not too busy.... Could I get a coffee?"

"Sure, sure, never too busy for you!"

Deanna smiled and glanced downward, repressing the urge to giggle at Paul's marijuana-infused brand of customer service. The jingling bell on the door caused her to look back up, and she found herself face to face with the BitterSweet Bistro's head bartender, Louis Miller. The smile Paul's antics had caused faded, and she tried to school her features into a poker face.

Louis Miller was probably the last person on Earth she would have liked to see at that moment.

He had been a friend and mentor to her at the BitterSweet, and somewhere along the way, she had developed a giant crush on him. It had not ended well, due largely to the issues Deanna was dealing with in her own mind at the time. She did not want to think about how she had behaved toward Lou shortly before leaving the BitterSweet. Seeing him, and feeling his judgements – whether they actually existed or not, she felt them - would not be helpful to getting her out of her winter funk.

He was right there, though, and looking right at her, so she didn't really see any other choice.

"Hello, Lou," she said, keeping her voice and countenance reserved.

"Hey, you," he responded lightly. "How are things in your world?"

Deanna shrugged, unwilling to admit she was pretty much failing at life. She was horrified to realize there were tears gathering behind her eyes.

"Here you go, Deanna," Paul interrupted. "Oh, hey, Lou! Hey, this must be like a reunion for you guys!"

The awkwardness in the air was so thick, Deanna thought she would choke on it, but Lou managed to power through. "It has been a while. Could I just get my usual, Paul?"

Paul scampered back through the curtain, leaving Lou and Deanna in awkward silence.

"So, anything new?" Deanna asked, in as casual a tone as she could muster.

"Not really. BitterSweet's still crazy, but good. And I'm doing a lot better," Lou responded, making Deanna remember things that made the tears behind her eyes threaten to spill over. "I'm going to meetings again. Got four months under my belt now."

"Good, good," she murmured in response. "I'm glad you're getting healthy."

"I really am," he expounded. "The bar is busier than ever, I'm working on my art, meditating every day… I feel like myself again for the first time in a long time."

"Guess sometimes you have to go through hell to see the face of God." Deanna was rather surprised to hear these words coming out of her own mouth, with no apparent input from her brain.

"Not sure I've seen the face of God," Lou said with a half-smile. "Just getting myself back on track."

"I've always imagined he looks like Tom Petty," she found herself blurting.

Lou's eyebrow shot up in response. She was glad his black-rimmed glasses hid a bit of the expression in his eyes, which she was certain, at this point, would be one of condemnation.

Lou's lips twitched for a moment, before he finally said, "Tom Petty?" with an amused air.

"Oh, yeah," Deanna said, trying to hide her embarrassment. "Almost every time I've had any kind of major epiphany or creative inspiration, Tom Petty was playing for some reason. So I've kind of come to the conclusion that God looks like Tom Petty."

"Makes perfect sense," Lou said, politely.

Deanna imagined he was probably thinking she should be committed. She had the sudden urge to flee.

"Well, I'd better run," she said aloud. "Things to do."

"It was good to see you, Deanna," Lou responded softly.

She fairly ran out of the café.

She knew she was being silly, but seeing Lou had been like being punched right in the self -esteem, when her self-esteem was just trying to get back up after some serious abuse. She tried to push the encounter out of her mind and think positive thoughts as she walked back toward the laundromat.

As she approached the laundromat, she noticed the robed man again, standing in the doorway of the apartment building next door. She nodded and smiled in greeting, and he murmured something quietly enough that she wasn't sure she heard him correctly. It sounded like, "Even a queen needs connection."

She wasn't entirely sure if that's what he said, and she wasn't sure if it was a pickup line, so she opted to pretend she had heard nothing as she entered the laundromat.

As she removed her clothes from the washer and loaded them into the dryer, she decided her next stop should be the library. A good book would take her mind off things.

David

He had no idea where he was. That was nothing new, obviously; it had been his general state of being for a very long time. However, this place seemed a bit different than any other place he had ever been.

He was standing on a sidewalk, surrounded by buildings and people who scurried past without paying him much attention. That was normal.

Every so often, though, a cold wind would blow and make him feel as if he could no longer stand. No one else on the street seemed affected. However, each time the cold wind picked up – which seemed to happen every few minutes – he was nearly paralyzed by feelings of cold and darkness. It was a fairly terrifying experience.

In between the winds, though, he saw and heard wonderful things. There was beautiful music playing, although he could not find its source, and all manner of people in colorful clothes. There was warm, golden sunlight in the sky, and a general sense of safety and contentment.

Until the winds struck, rendering him powerless for seconds or even minutes at a time.

After one such wind subsided, he turned a corner and saw a beautifully carved gargoyle statue on a bench. As he walked toward it, it took a long sip out of a cup in its hand, and waved at him. He wasn't sure he had ever seen such a thing, so he stopped and stared. A moment later, the gargoyle proffered his cup and said, "You want a sip, man? Nice warm cocoa. Cure for what ails you."

He reached for the cup, somewhat timidly, and took a tiny sip. The hot, sweet beverage tasted like safety and happiness. He closed his eyes in happiness while he swallowed it, then offered it back to the gargoyle, who casually waved it away and smiled, saying, "I can get more at the community center. You enjoy."

David nodded and walked down the street, taking tiny sips of the cocoa as he walked. He wanted to make it last. He couldn't remember the last time he felt so comforted, so safe.

Something clicked in what was left of his mind. This cocoa tasted like something in his mantra.

"Find a world where I can be safe."

The delicious, hot beverage definitely heightened this feeling of safety, but he realized he had been feeling that way for a while. He wasn't quite sure when it had started. Vague images and feelings

15

flickered through his broken mind. There was a lady, he thought. A nice lady. She had told him he could go and be safe in this world, and even have a nice day. It had been a long time since he'd had a really nice day.

He smiled, and sipped his cocoa. He couldn't be certain if he was truly safe, but the cocoa was the best thing he had tasted in a long, long time.

Back on the Main Street, Deanna nodded and smiled at a few passersby that she recognized from around town. She passed the Piano Man, his fingers wiggling in the air as he played an unheard sonata. She greeted him, neither expecting nor receiving an answer; however, he appeared to watch her walk by, which was a tad unnerving. He never usually looked at anyone.

As she entered the library, the heavyset, grey-haired woman behind the desk smiled and said, "There she is! Haven't seen you in a while."

"You weren't here last time I was in, Barb," Deanna replied.

"Oh, must've been a Tuesday. That's my day off. You ready for tonight?"

Deanna stared blankly at her. "Tonight?"

"Buh – buh – buh – buuuuh," the librarian sang dramatically. "SNOWMAGEDDON! They're calling for like, two feet."

"I heard eight inches."

"Nope, two feet or more," Barb replied earnestly.

"Uh-huh, sure. You believe that, I've got a bridge to sell you. Remember the last 'snowmageddon'?" Deanna referred to the storm they were supposed to get a few weeks earlier, for which the governor had called a state of emergency and many businesses had closed early. The storm had missed them, giving them only a light dusting of snow, and leaving a lot of people very disgruntled toward meteorologists.

"Well, it snowed like the dickens, just not here. Beat the hell out of Boston," Barb said. "My daughter lives up there, she still hasn't dug her car out. So you be prepared, get some good books and hit the grocery store. Get yourself some movies, too." The librarian gestured at the wall of DVD's, in the center of which a TV was mounted. It was currently playing the movie, *The Matrix*, though it was near the end of the film.

"Don't you ever get tired of watching this, Barb?"

"I could never get tired of Keanu! He really is the one!" the librarian said, laughing as she quoted the movie. The two women watched as Keanu Reeves's character, Neo, stopped a hail of bullets with the power of his mind, marking his acceptance of his role as "The One" who would save the world.

After they watched for a few moments, Barb seemed to snap out of her Keanu-fueled reverie. "Hey, we've got that Discworld book you were looking for," she said, bringing her attention back to reality.

"Really, you got *The Shepherd's Crown*?" Deanna was elated; it was the only book of Terry Pratchett's Discworld series she had not yet read. The author, a lifelong favorite of hers, had passed away months earlier, and the book was published posthumously.

"Yep, it's on the shelf. Go to town."

Deanna thanked her and scurried over to the Fiction section, grabbing the Pratchett book off the shelf as if someone were going to beat her to it if she wasn't quick enough. Then she pored through each shelf, as she always did, looking for titles to jump out at her and promise to give her the mental vacation good books always provided.

She had read everything they had by most of her favorite authors, like Neil Gaiman, Charles DeLint, and Jim Butcher, but she found one by Jonathan Carroll and another by Christopher Moore that she had not yet read. She loved the fantasy genre. Since she had been a small child, she had secret faith that magic was real and the things that happened in fantasy books could happen in real life.

Once, she read a quote online by author Charles DeLint. "That's the thing about magic," the quote had read. "You have to know that it's here, it's all around us, or it just stays invisible to you." The quote gelled with her worldview; deep down, she truly, deeply believed that magic was all around, even though she had seen no hard evidence of that fact. She had played around with Wicca as a teenager, and things of that nature, but saw no great results with her spells. She had been to a variety of churches and experimented with various faiths, and though she had never witnessed an honest-to-God miracle, she remained undeterred in her belief that one could occur at any moment. Somehow, she just knew there was a mysterious, benevolent force at work in the universe, whether it was magical or mystical or spiritual, or all three.

She rarely discussed these beliefs with anyone, lest she be deemed insane and watched with careful eyes or worse, locked away in some kind of facility. Deanna knew she wasn't crazy, though. On the contrary, these quiet beliefs in magic and greater mysteries often helped to keep her sane in the face of constant financial worries and seemingly never-ending excruciating minutiae of the mundane world most accept as "reality."

The fantasy-fiction genre allowed her to suspend any disbelief and cynicism life had attempted to instill in her and rest securely in stories of magic and happy endings. Reading such books provided a necessary break from the harsh realities of adulthood and stoked the fire of her belief in miraculous possibilities.

While she inspected each shelf, Deanna remembered the first time she had read a book from Terry Pratchett's Discworld series. It was more than twenty years ago, when she was sixteen. Adolescence had been very hard for her. She didn't have any close friends, and felt terribly alone; she hated herself, and her internal dialogue was a never ending stream of self-directed venom. She wound up trying to kill herself, and her parents, not knowing how else to help her, brought her to a mental hospital. The Discworld book, *The Color of Magic*, had been in the hospital's library, and she read it three times over the course of the next month. It distracted her from the abyss of depression and self-loathing that had only been exacerbated by her failed attempt at suicide.

Now, in the library, Deanna shook her head gently as if to dislodge the memory. She wondered why it had popped into her mind at all. It was not a period of her life she enjoyed dwelling on, and she generally avoided thinking about it.

A young man entered the aisle in which she stood and she looked up at him, welcoming the distraction from her own, loud thoughts. Idly, she noticed that he was attractive; roughly ten years her junior, tall, and well built, with blonde hair and intensely blue eyes which were currently focused on the books on the shelf. He wore all black, and seemed completely oblivious to her presence.

Though she knew the idea was ridiculous, she couldn't help feeling that he was invading her privacy. She had had carte blanche of the entire fiction section, and now she had to work around him. She sighed, and decided to be grateful for the distraction from her unhappy memories rather than annoyed by the intrusion on her personal space. Having made this decision, she attempted to re-engross herself in looking through book titles.

Though she actively tried to block out his existence from her awareness, the good looking guy was creeping down the aisle, too engrossed in reading book spines to notice Deanna. As he encroached further and further into her personal space, she found it more and more difficult to ignore his presence. Finally, his elbow bumped her arm and she said, "Pardon me," though it was clearly not her fault.

When she spoke, the guy gasped and twitched as if she had snuck up behind him and jabbed a knife into his ribs. At first, Deanna thought he was just startled because he hadn't noticed she was there, but when he turned to face her, all of the color drained from his face. He stared at her with wide eyes as if she was the monster under his bed from childhood, with spiders coming out of her eyes, and two guns pointed at him. He was breathing fast and hard; he was *terrified.*

"Are you okay?" she asked as gently as she could, wondering if he was having an anxiety attack or something.

He appeared to be catching his breath, at least. That was good. However, the apparent fear in his eyes had not dimmed at all.

Then he whispered with apparent shock, "You can see me."

"Well, yes," Deanna said, trying her best not to sound as if she were talking to an imbecile. She wondered if he had something wrong with him, or if he was on something. "You're right in front of me."

He reached into his pocket and pulled out a device that looked like an iPhone 6s. It was larger than many cell phones, but not obscenely so. He held the device toward her while staring at the screen with narrowed eyes, looking as if he were trying to figure out a problem. In an attempt to alleviate the intense awkwardness she was feeling, Deanna asked, "New phone?"

He made an exasperated sound and stared at her, looking irritated. "Why can you see me?" he almost hissed. "Are you with Carver?"

"Um…" if Deanna wasn't already nearly backed into the bookshelf, she would have backed away further; as it was, she really had no escape. She tried to keep her voice gentle as she said, "Again, you're right in front of me. My eyes work. So I can see you. I'm gonna go now, though, so calm down. This aisle is all yours."

She tried to step around him but he blocked her path, so she put a hand on his arm and pushed gently. It was more a gesture than an actual push, to show she was trying to get around him, but he steadfastly refused to move, so she put a little more muscle into the gesture. However, he was about six inches taller and quite a bit heavier than she, and he did not budge an inch. She may as well have been trying to push the bookshelf out of the way, for all the good it did. Fear was starting to flutter around in her chest like a caged bird as she assessed the situation and realized a potential lunatic had her backed into the wall, trapped, and there was no one else in the fiction section.

He stared at her hand on his arm while she tried to push him away, then his hand snapped up and wrapped around her neck. She gasped for breath as he growled, "How are you doing this?" For a second, she was mute with terror; then, she tried to scream. It was, quite literally, a strangled sound, and it ended quickly as he squeezed her neck tighter, but it was enough to be heard in the mostly-empty, quiet library. She could hear Barb's footsteps hurrying over from the front desk as the older woman called, "You okay, honey? What's wrong?"

The man in black let go and took a step back, leaving Deanna pale and shaking. As the librarian rushed into the aisle and toward her, the words, "Call the police!" were forming behind Deanna's lips. She never got to say it, though, as she was shocked into silence when Barb stepped right through the man, as if he weren't even there. There was no special effect, he didn't go transparent like a ghost in the movies; Barb just walked forward and put her hands on Deanna's shoulders, never giving any sign that she was aware of anyone else in the aisle.

"Honey, what's wrong? Do you need a doctor?"

Deanna stared, wide-eyed, over the librarian's head at the man in black. She could not comprehend what had just happened. "Barb…" she began, trying to figure out what to say. "Barb, did you see that man in black?"

The librarian looked around for a moment before saying quietly, "Honey, nobody else is here." Deanna continued to stare over Barb's head at the man behind her; the librarian took her silence and lack of eye contact as a sign that she was having a heart attack or something like it, so the older woman said, "I'll be right back, honey, I'm calling an ambulance. You're going to be okay."

As Barb scurried back to the front desk to make the call, moving much faster than a woman of her size and age should be able to move, Deanna sunk to the floor, in shock. She stared up at the man in black, wondering if he really was there or if she had finally, truly lost her mind. She whispered, "What the hell is going on?"

"I was kind of hoping you would tell me," he said, squatting in front of her. "I guess we should talk."

Steven

Ensign Steven Drisbane was enjoying his assignment in Woodford. It certainly wasn't what he had expected when he enlisted in the United States Navy, seven long years ago.

He had been nineteen at the time, and had no idea at all what he wanted to do with his life. He knew he didn't want to work some dead-end, minimum wage job, nor did he feel any interest in any kind of career involving physical labor. He figured he should go to college, but didn't have a strong enough interest in any particular subject to get him truly motivated toward going that route. Thus, when his little sister said she was going to join the navy after she finished high school, he decided he would do the same. They could learn the ropes together.

When his sister turned eighteen, she changed her mind about joining the navy. It was too late, though; Steven had already enlisted.

He didn't really mind. Boot camp was obviously no picnic, and he would have liked a little more time to relax, but the Navy made him feel as if he were actually doing something with his life. He had no intention of making a career out of it, at first. He figured he would just put in his four years and get college paid for, end of story.

In his third year in the Navy, he had been working as a meteorologist in Virginia. Basically, he looked at a computer screen all day, identifying weather patterns that might affect ships at sea. It was a mellow assignment with relatively easy work, which suited him fine.

One day, though, he noticed something odd. The Doppler Lidar, which measured the frequency of backscattered light from a laser in order to measure temperature and wind speed, was giving some very strange readings in a certain section of the Pacific Ocean. He checked all of the other available equipment readings for that area, and found nothing odd. *Something* was interfering with the Lidar, though; he had never before seen readings like that. He reported it to his commanding officer, who told him he'd get the equipment checked.

Not long after that, Steven received notice that he was being reassigned. There were no further details given; he was simply given an official letter that said to report to an office that he had never before been to the following morning. He had never heard of such a quick and mysterious reassignment, but he had learned not to question orders rather early on in his military career. Also, he figured even if he hated the new assignment, he had less than a year left in the navy. It would go by quickly.

So, he reported to that mysterious office not far from where he had been doing his meteorology work, and he waited. He waited for the better part of an hour, alone, until two men – they looked like Captains to him, though the insignias they wore were somehow slightly different than any he had seen before – entered the office through a previously unnoticed back door. There were no formal introductions, nor did the men offer any further explanation. The officer on the right instructed Steven to sit at the only desk in the room, gave him a written test, and told him he had an hour to complete it. After that, there was another test; after that, another.

The tests themselves shed no light on his situation. The first seemed like a combination of an IQ test and a psychological exam. The second (which the officer on the left gave him, with an allotted time of one hour to complete) was a test of his meteorological knowledge, but some of the questions were almost nonsensical. They seemed to focus largely on light refraction and sound waves, which was fine, but they asked about possibilities that did not exist, readings that could not exist. He remembered the strange lidar readings, and answered to the best of his ability, thinking all the while that he was being set up for something unpleasant. Anxiety began to permeate the very core of his being; try as he might, he could not still his twitching limbs. He tried to focus on the tests themselves without worrying about the reasons behind them or the consequences they could bring him.

The third test, however, was simply laughable. The officer on the right (whom Steven had begun to think of as Captain Righty, as opposed to his partner, Captain Lefty) gave him the test and said, "forty minutes." He flipped it open.

The first section showed pictures of strange symbols, the likes of which he had never seen, and asked him to describe what they might mean. In the second section, he was asked to solve equations which featured more completely alien symbols. After staring at each question in disbelief, Steven would write down a number, or even another equation; these answers were pure guesses, jotted down more because he thought they looked nice there than for any logical reason. Once or twice, he just copied the symbol from one equation as the answer to another.

He started to think this was all some elaborate practical joke; however, the two officers who stood nearby never cracked a smile or, for that matter, spoke a word while he took his tests. They would simply give him each test and tell him how much time he had to take it, and then stand silently. Silently and, he thought, rather menacingly.

Finally, in the third section, he was asked to describe any "unexplainable and unusual experiences" he had had both in the Navy and in his civilian life before enlisting.

For lack of a better answer, he described the odd lidar readings as his "unexplainable" Navy experience, though he felt like writing a detailed account of the test he was currently taking. It seemed a far more "unexplainable and unusual experience."

He considered whether he had had any such experiences in his civilian life, and drew a blank. Just as he was about to throw in the towel, he remembered something:

He was ten years old, visiting an aunt in Pennsylvania with his mother. He was outside playing, and he heard a loud motorcycle engine coming down the usually quiet road. He watched it go past; a shiny, gleaming black and silver machine that made him wish he was old enough to have one. It stopped suddenly, made a quick U-turn, and drew to a stop right in front of Steven, maybe five feet away. The driver removed his helmet and stared silently but intently at him for several seconds. The biker was a small but muscular man who looked to be in his early fifties, with dark skin and a few grey hairs. He was dressed all in black. Steven wished his mom or aunt would come out of the house; this man's dark eyes scared him. Even at ten years old, Steven knew when he looked into the biker's eyes that something was very wrong in the man's mind. Steven did not speak. He was made mute by terror, wondering what the man would do next. He thought he might be kidnapped or worse. Then, with no explanation, the biker said, "That's not how you treat the Lady, friend." Then, he put his helmet back on and drove away, just as suddenly as he had appeared.

Steven remembered this, and wrote a brief synopsis of the experience on the last page of the test. He had no idea if it was the kind of answer they were looking for, but it was the only thing that had come to mind.

The officers took all three of his tests and instructed him to wait where he was. He sat at the desk, worried and waiting, for another hour. He began to feel he would never see the light of day again.

Then, the officers returned. Captain Righty said, "We've reviewed your tests. Pack your belongings and meet us here at 0600 tomorrow. You will be relocated."

Steven did as he was told. He didn't have much to pack; it only took him an hour or so. He did not (could not) sleep that night.

The next morning, he returned to the office, carrying all of his belongings. The two officers met him outside and loaded his things into a black SUV, then told him to get in the backseat. The two of them got in front. Lefty drove. No one spoke. Steven made a few attempts at lighthearted conversation about the weather and such, but neither Righty nor Lefty responded to anything he said with any more than a perfunctory nod.

The drive went on for hours. At some point, Steven fell asleep. When he awoke, he was still in the backseat of the silent vehicle. He felt horribly disoriented. Only by looking out the window and studying the signs did he figure out that they were in Connecticut. The car showed no signs of stopping. More time passed; between the silence in the car and not knowing where their destination was, it felt like an eternity.

Finally, about two hours after they passed a "Welcome to Maine" sign, the SUV left the highway and turned down a series of exponentially more rural side roads. The last road onto which they turned was neither paved nor even gravel, simply a long stretch of dirt and grass with vague indications of tire marks. After about half a mile, they reached a large clearing in which there stood three rather nondescript, brick-faced buildings. They looked small warehouses or large offices; Steven could not decide which.

The SUV parked by the door of the middle building. Other vehicles of similar make and model were parked around all three buildings. However, there were no signs of life, no indications of who might drive those vehicles.

Lefty and Righty got out of the car first. Steven followed them awkwardly. His legs and back were sore from sitting in the cramped backseat for so long, and he did not know what was expected of him. "Should I bring my things?" he asked.

"Not yet," Righty responded, a tad curtly.

Lefty swiped some kind of identification card to enter the building. Inside, a short hallway brought them to a second door; this time, Righty swiped a card to get in. They walked through a drab hallway lined with closed doors. At a seemingly arbitrary door, they stopped. Lefty extracted a key from his pocket, opened the door, and told Steven, "Wait in there for the General."

Steven blinked, confused. "General" was not a rank used in the Navy. It was an Army rank, he believed; the Navy equivalent would be an Admiral. He opened his mouth to voice his confusion, but Righty put a hand on his back and pushed him, gently but firmly, into the room. The door closed behind him; he knew even before he tried the handle that it would be locked from the outside. He was not wrong.

The room in which he was now essentially imprisoned was about 8' by 10', and entirely done in a very dark grey. The walls, the carpeting, the two uncomfortable-looking chairs and the small, round table between them – all that same shade of dark, almost charcoal grey. There were two panels of fluorescent lights in the tiled ceiling (the tiles were also grey); all of the dark grey coloring seemed to absorb the light. There were no windows. Steven prowled around the small room like a caged animal. "Righty and Lefty's uniforms were wrong," he thought. "I couldn't even tell for sure what their rank was. And now I'm waiting for a "general"? Have I been kidnapped? Is this all some elaborate hoax? What is going on?" His thoughts chased each other around his head, sending panic waves throughout his body. His heart was beating too fast, his head was pounding. He realized he was having an anxiety attack. The realization did not make him feel any better.

By the time he heard the door handle turning, Steven was near hyperventilation and clammy with cold sweat. He stood at attention as the door opened, more because he didn't know what else to do than out of any sense of duty. A short, stocky man with grey hair and wire-rimmed glasses entered the room and closed the door behind him. With a vague wave of the clipboard in his hand, the man said, "No need for all that, Drisbane. Sit." Steven did so.

The older man looked down at Steven, and was apparently startled by what he saw. "Good heavens, man. Are you alright? Here, drink this." He handed Steven a bottle of water that he had been carrying, which was received gratefully. As Steven sipped the water and tried to focus on breathing normally, the other man sat in the chair opposite him. They looked at each other across the small, round table, sizing each other up.

The older man was not wearing any kind of uniform Steven had ever seen. He wore all black. Black boots, black pants, black button-down shirt, black pea coat with strange, matte black insignias on the lapel. His face was not unfriendly, and his blue eyes glittered with a kind of jovial intensity that made him look like he was thinking of a really funny joke that he was simply too busy to share at the moment. After a small eternity (to Steven...in actuality, about sixty seconds passed), the man spoke.

"So, Steven Drisbane. I'm General Larsen. I'm sure you have plenty of questions for me, but first I have a few for you. First off, have you ever had any experiences with magic?"

Steven made an unsuccessful attempt to choke back the surprised laughter that bubbled up. It came out as a snort, followed by a high-pitched giggle. Larsen waited patiently for an answer without any change in facial expression.

"Have I ever...what?" The last syllable came out about seven octaves higher than Steven's normal speaking voice.

"Have you ever had any experiences with magic?" Larsen repeated, with a tone that seemed to suggest it was the most logical question in the world. Steven actually guffawed. He had previously only read about people guffawing in books, but there was no other way to describe the sound that escaped his lips. Larsen continued staring at him with a serious, though not unfriendly, expression. The man was not joking. Steven tried to think of an answer that would not involve cursing the other man out or laughing hysterically.

"I mean.... I've read the Harry Potter books. Watched the Lord of the Rings trilogy many times. But outside of the world of fiction, no, I can't say I have ever had any experiences with magic."

"That's because all of the energy described as 'magic' has been contained," Larsen stated. "It is contained, controlled, and has been studied for a number of years. Quite a useful tool, though a bit unpredictable."

"Ah...," Steven simply could not find words to say. He was dumbfounded. The only clear thought in his mind was, "This has to be a joke."

"Of course," Larsen continued, "harnessing this energy, studying it, controlling it, and using it for the greater good of our great country takes a lot of manpower. It takes a unique mind to be up to the challenge. Now tell me, what was unique about the lidar readings you reported to your commanding officer?"

"Well sir, I had just never seen readings like that before. The light frequency was just... it was just wrong."

"What if I told you that the readings were picking up a discharge of magical energy?"

"I... I would find it difficult to believe, sir," Steven replied hesitantly.

"Of course you would, you're a logical man. Now tell me, what were your thoughts on the third test you were given yesterday?"

"It was… well," Steven stammered. "It was a bit difficult to understand. I didn't recognize any of the symbols."

"And yet you scored quite well," Larsen said smoothly. "Finally, tell me more about the biker you encountered when you were a child. That was… let me see," he shuffled through some papers on his clipboard. "That was 1998, correct?"

"Yes… yes sir. I was ten. Um…. The guy just drove by, turned around, pulled up in front of me, and told me, 'That's not how you treat the lady, friend,' then drove off."

"Did he specifically say, 'the Lady,' or did he say 'a lady'?"

"The Lady. I'm sure about that. It confused me, trying to figure out who he meant."

"What do you think he meant by that statement?"

"I honestly have no idea. I mean, there was no lady present. My mom and aunt were inside. I was ten. I have no idea what he was talking about."

"What did the man look like?"

"Uhhhh… he was black. Small guy, but looked like he was in good shape. Had on black clothes."

Larsen nodded as if satisfied. He removed a photograph from the jumble of papers on his clipboard and put it on the table in front of Steven. "Was that the man you saw?"

Steven studied the picture. His memory of that day was fourteen years old but still quite vivid. The man in the picture looked almost exactly like the man he had seen; short hair shot with grey, black clothes. The eyes, however, looked a little different. Not as frightening as Steven remembered. "It looks like him, sir. But the eyes are wrong. Less… dark. He had very dark eyes. Not just the color, they looked kind of… haunted, I guess. His eyes scared me."

Larsen nodded again. "Why did you choose that experience when asked about unexplainable and unusual experiences?"

"It just popped into my head," Steven confessed. "I didn't know what else to put."

"Good, good," Larsen said while he scribbled some notes on a paper Steven could not see. "Now, Mr. Drisbane, I'd imagine you have some questions for me. You may ask them."

A thousand questions were screaming in Steven's mind, but he started with the most recent query to join the bunch. "Why do you have a photograph of a man I saw for about thirty seconds when I was a kid?"

"Excellent question. That man is Chief Admiral David Carver. He founded our organization, about forty years ago. He deserted his post about fourteen years ago. I believe you saw him days after his desertion, though he may have been operating within a different timeline than you or me."

Though Steven was confused by the General's comment about a timeline, he decided it would make more sense to respond to the issue that made more sense in his worldview. "Chief Admiral…. That's a Navy rank," he pointed out. "'General' is not. I'm a little confused by your rank, sir."

"Excellent observation."

Several long, awkward, silent seconds passed before Steven hesitantly asked, "Could you… could you explain why your rank is general?"

"Ah, of course. You just need to ask, boy. I'm a general because I've been in the army a very long time and done my job well," Larsen stated plainly.

"You're in…. the army?"

"Of course."

Steven stared blankly at him for several long seconds. "I'm… I'm Navy."

"Yes, I know."

Again, several long seconds passed while the two men stared at each other in silence. Larsen looked totally sincere and unperturbed. Steven tried to figure out how to proceed. Finally, he said, "Am I being reassigned to work with you?"

"Yes."

"And… How would our working relationship be defined?"

"I'd be your general," Larsen said with maddening simplicity.

Steven pinched the bridge of his nose to try to ward off the pressure that was building in his temples. "Why would I, as a naval petty officer third class, have an army general to report to?"

"Ahhhh, good one. The truth of it is, our organization has recruited men and women from all branches of the military, and even a few non-military types who know their stuff really well or provide some kind unique service or asset to us. But most of us are military. Since our true work is not public knowledge, we keep everyone's ranks from their former positions, and promote them in accordance with the ranks of their branch of the military. This way, we can tell our families about promotions and whatnot without letting on about the true nature of our organization."

Steven mulled this over. "What, exactly, is the true nature of the organization?"

"I thought I'd explained. We study the contained energy that could be called 'magic.' We find uses for it. We keep it safe, and we harness it for the greater good of our country."

"And... what will my role be?"

"As far as anyone else knows, you are working in another meteorology station. But in reality, to start, your role will be student. You have a lot to learn, our training program takes about two years. Consider yourself re-enlisted. Now, come. I will show you to your quarters. Get a good night's sleep. Your lessons begin at 0700 tomorrow."

So Steven became a student.

He learned, over the next two years, that magic was incredibly responsive to belief. The actual molecular energy would transmutate in reaction to certain beliefs, or lack of belief. Therefore, someone who didn't believe in magic would never actually see magic, in its raw state. The organization, in containing the energy and using it as a tool of sorts – a fuel for their technological tools, really – had found ways to keep it "sanitized," unaffected by belief.

He learned that the color black attracted natural energy, and that energy could be used to boost the magical energy that powered their technological instruments. For that reason, all of the organization's uniforms were black.

He learned that many magic-powered tools had been invented and developed by the organization for which he now worked. Specifically, they had been invented by Chief Admiral David Carver. The man had apparently started out as an old-school practitioner of magic, engaged in occult dealings and elaborate rituals. Somehow, over time, he had figured out how to isolate the magical energy and use it to power technological devices that made it accessible to the common man. He had enlisted the help of others, of inventors and soldiers and anyone else he could find. They had tweaked, streamlined, and upgraded the devices as new technologies were developed. Eventually, the government began subsidizing the development.

It started as a small group. Carver hand selected a few people to help him bring his ideas to life. Then, as their budget grew and the government's interest in their work heightened, they started bringing in more experts and using their inventions to serve the greater good of their country. They set up shop in Maine, and enlisted people from various branches of the military. The organization was formed.

Many of the original devices invented by Carver were still used by the organization, and Steven learned to use them well. One such instrument, sardonically called "the Wand," was standard issue for all operatives. It had the power to alter molecules and transform existing reality and even to track individual molecules, among other things. If one wished it, they could use their Wand (which was actually a small, rectangular device that looked not unlike a smart phone) to make someone invisible; they could then use the Wand to find the invisible person, wherever they might be.

Another instrument, given the witty moniker "the Broom," allowed agents to travel hundreds of miles within seconds just by pushing a button.

Steven learned to use such devices with skill, and how to live as an operative in such a secret organization. He learned the importance of secrecy, and of dedication to furthering the cause of using accessible magic to support the greater good.

Mostly, though, he learned a lot about Chief Admiral David Carver.

Carver, as Steven would learn, had deserted his post sixteen years before Steven started his training. He had gotten the organization up and running, invented the basic tools they used and inspired them to continue the work, and then he had simply, inexplicably disappeared. It was said that he had become more and more withdrawn in his last few years before deserting, isolating himself completely from his fellow operatives. His behavior became odd and erratic. He would disappear for long lengths of time, and come back... changed. He would never tell any of his operatives details about where he went during these disappearances, only saying he was gathering data.

His eyes told a different story though, as they grew more haunted and more distant with each disappearance. He seemed to be slipping into a dark, lonely world, and no one knew how to reach out to him and bring him back to their reality. Some pontificated that all of his work with the magical energy was backfiring, and the energy was somehow taking him over. He did not share what went on in his mind, though, so no one knew for certain.

During his last weeks in Maine, Carver's behavior became utterly incomprehensible. He would scream at operatives for things that they had not yet done. He would leave a meeting to go to the men's room, and call thirty minutes later from Australia, uncertain how he got there. It was as if he had some strange, magical version of Alzheimer's, with all of the confusion but none of the constraints of time and space. No one in the organization knew how to deal with it.

Then, one day, he just vanished. They searched for him, of course. They searched the entire planet, using their Wands and every trick they knew. Occasionally, they would pick up a faint trace of his unique energy readings, which they called an energy signature. It was never more than a trace, though, and never enough to follow. It was unknown whether Chief Admiral David Carver even still walked the earth. Various operatives presented long, involved theories hypothesizing that Carver had gotten lost in some unknown dimension, or that he had actually died. No one could prove any of these theories beyond all reasonable doubt.

But the organization lived on.

After Steven had studied for two years, he was sworn in as an officer of the organization. The oath was not terribly different than the one he had taken when he joined the Navy. He was being promoted to ensign, though, so he took The Oath of Office for officers, which was slightly different than the original oath he had taken. Also, with the organization being what it was, there were a few practical modifications.

In front of a panel of commanding officers and alongside several other new officers, Steven raised his right hand and swore: "I, Ensign Steven Drisbane, having been appointed an officer in the Navy of the United States, as indicated in the above grade of ensign, do solemnly affirm that I will support and defend the Constitution of the United States against all enemies, foreign or domestic, from this plane of reality or any other; that I will bear true faith and allegiance to the same, that I take this obligation freely, without any mental reservations, under no magical influence, and with no purpose of evasion, and that I will well and faithfully discharge the duties of the office upon which I am about to enter. So help me God."

(The parts that mentioned specific rank and branch were a little garbled, as the new officers, from various branches of the armed forces, took the oath in unison.)

Steven wasn't an overly emotional young man, but as he took the oath, he had a tear in his eye. His chest swelled with pride. He had come to truly love the organization and their work; it made him feel as if he had finally found out the secrets of life he always suspected were there. He loved being separate from the mundane world, from ordinary people with their boring, trivial lives. He could actually use magic, with the purpose of protecting and improving his country. It was like a boyhood daydream come true. He felt like a superhero.

Once he was sworn in, Steven would be given his first assignment. He was so excited to find out what it would be that he could barely stand it. However, there was a small reception first (at least they served lunch – free food went a long way toward helping him push aside his impatience); by the time the two hour event ended, Steven's leg was involuntarily twitching with sheer anticipation.

Finally, after the festivities, one of the organization's Generals handed out black envelopes to the new officers. Each of them opened their envelope, read the paper inside, and burst into excited chatter. All around, young officers were gleefully shouting things like, "I'm going to be a Wand specialist!" and, "I'm an energy tracker!" and even, "I've got 'boogie man' patrol!" (There was no actual boogie man; 'boogie man patrol' was the organization's amusing nickname for the task force assigned to prevent negative backlash when magical energy was discharged. The energy, in its raw state, worked by the Golden Rule philosophy, "What you put out will be returned to you threefold." The Boogie Man Patrol used technological development to prevent this from happening at inconvenient times.) Everyone seemed very pleased... except for Steven. He wordlessly stared at his paper as if waiting for the words typed on it to change.

One of the other new officers noticed, and said, "What's wrong, Drisbane? Where'd they stick you?"

Steven shrugged, and walked away. The organization had taught him discretion. He saw no reason to tell the other new officers that his paper said only, "Room 301, 6:00 tonight."

At 5:59 pm, he knocked on the door of room 301. At precisely 6:00 pm, it opened. General Larsen was nothing if not absolutely literal.

"Come in, Drisbane, have a seat," the General said as he ushered Steven into a room nearly identical to that in which they had had their first meeting. They both wore the standard black uniforms this time, but Steven's sense of confusion and dread felt all too familiar.

"Why was I not given an assignment, General?"

"You were. You just weren't given a paper explaining your assignment."

Now that he was quite used to Larsen's ways, Steven followed up with another direct question.

"Why was I not given a paper explaining my assignment?"

"Ah. That is an excellent question. You're quite good at asking excellent questions, have I ever told you that? Well, now I have." Larsen shuffled through some papers on the table in front of him. "You were not given a paper, Drisbane, because you are being given a special assignment, the likes of which the organization has not embarked upon in the past."

"I...wow," Steven said, nonplussed. "Doing what, exactly?"

"You are going to find David Carver and bring him in by any means necessary."

Steven blinked several times. "David Carver? Chief Admiral David Carver? The founder? I thought he was dead, or in another dimension or something."

"Those are rumors. We know that he is alive. For the past couple of years, there have been more and more traces of his molecular structure and energy signature picked up by our equipment. He never stays in one place long enough for us to catch up to him, and we cannot seem to predict where he will turn up next." Larsen sighed. "For over a decade, he was either laying low or simply … not himself. We have seen more evidence of him in the past year than we have in the past decade as a whole."

"If this has been going on for over a year, why wait 'til now to bring him in? Why didn't you track him down a year ago?"

"Couple of reasons. First, we needed to train the right candidate to catch the man. It may not be as simple as finding him and bringing him here. He may not be the same man he was before he left. It's been a very long time."

"What makes me the right candidate?"

"Honestly? There have been too many 'coincidences' involving you and him. I have learned, in my years on this earth, that there is no such thing as coincidence. You actually met Carver, albeit briefly, just as

34

he was deserting his post. Then, by a completely unrelated string of so-called 'coincidences,' you caught the attention of the organization and joined us, yourself. While you were taking your entry exams, you inexplicably felt the desire to describe your meeting with Carver, even though you had no idea who he was or what it meant. That's too much 'coincidence,' if you ask me. It means something. I think there's a good chance you will be the man to find him."

Steven's ego deflated a bit that the General hadn't said something more grandiose, something along the lines of, "We've been waiting for a man with your talents!" However, he did his best to hide his disappointment.

"Has anyone been looking for him? Were you just waiting to assign me to the task?"

Larsen sighed, then, and looked uncharacteristically melancholy. He was silent for a long moment before saying, quite unexpectedly, "You know next year will be thirty years I'm with the organization?"

"I didn't know that, sir. Congratulations."

Larsen snorted. "When I first signed on, Carver was not just a great guy, but a genius. He was my friend, my teacher. I watched him deteriorate over time, just totally lose control..."

General Larsen paused for a long moment, apparently lost in memory. He stared at nothing in particular on the wall; his eyes, normally such a bright and jovial blue, looked nearly grey and somewhat glazed.

The moment passed, and he visibly shook himself. His gaze returned to Steven as he mentally returned to the present moment. "To answer your original question, many of us searched for him for years, when he first disappeared. That search dwindled as years dragged on, until it was just me looking in earnest. The only hard evidence I've ever found of his continued existence was his motorcycle, cast off and out of gas, abandoned in the Midwest." He sighed. "I've taken good care of it, in case he comes back. But that was nearly fifteen years ago. Since then, we have yet to pick up more than vague, ephemeral evidence, traces of his energy signature and so on. I've recruited some men from NASA to help improve our technology to find him, and we've picked up more and more energy signatures, but nothing concrete." He sighed again. "However, as we've found more and more of such traces, you've completed your training. Another coincidence. That's why I'm betting on you. Maybe you'll be the one to find him. "

Steven considered all that he had just learned.

"You said I will bring him in 'by any means necessary,' General. Are we treating Carver as an enemy? I understand your desire to find him, but 'by any means necessary' could be a bit drastic."

Larsen hesitated for a second before answering. "Carver is a threat to us, Ensign." (Steven felt a moment's pleasure at his superior's use of his new title.) "He is a threat to all of us. He knows all there is to know about us – possibly more than anyone currently with the organization; damn it, he WAS the organization – and he's unstable. Unpredictable. Out of control. Essentially, that makes him a dangerous weapon. Best case, he's just crazy – that still makes him the equivalent of a malfunctioning nuclear bomb that may or may not go off at any second. Worst case..."

The General paused, momentarily appearing much older than his fifty-five years.

"I truly want to believe that he is still the man I called a friend, but the fact is, he deserted fifteen years ago. It seemed like he had some kind of debilitating mental illness – it seemed like he had some kind of magical Alzheimer's, really. But what if he didn't? What if he did go crazy, but not the way we all thought? What if he deserted because he was against us? What if he turned against our country?" Larsen pounded a hand on the table. "We can't take the chance, Drisbane. We need him contained. He is a threat to all that we are. He could be a threat to civilians, too, if he's gone renegade. He could be a threat to civilians even if he's just crazy! Best case, worst case....whatever happens... Carver being out there, in the world... one way or the other, it has to stop."

Steven pondered the gravity of the situation, and the possible danger. After a moment, he nodded. "I'm your man, sir. How are we going to do things differently than you did on your previous attempts to find him?"

"Well, for one thing," Larsen replied, "we're gonna make damn sure he doesn't see you coming."

And so it was that Steven Drisbane became, quite literally, an invisible man. The tech operatives that Larsen had recruited from NASA, John and Eric, had tweaked Wands to keep Steven utterly invisible at all times. These upgraded Wands rendered him not only physically invisible, but undetectable by magical means. His very molecules were hidden to a point of near non-existence. The energy he emitted through the sheer act of living could not be picked up by man or machine. Even if he were to walk up to someone and punch them, while cloaked, the other person would not feel it; they may wonder why they had a vague soreness around the jaw, if they noticed anything at all. Steven's very matter was altered. He could not be heard, felt, smelled, or otherwise detected by any living creature while he was on the job, and he was always on the job.

Because of the myriad concealing powers of his new, improved Wand, Steven communicated with General Larsen only through typed messages – like text messages – and photographs sent via the Wand. Because of this new feature, and the Wand's general aesthetic similarity to a smartphone, Eric and John named the souped-up device the "SmartWand."

Steven had met the techs shortly after Larsen explained his new assignment. They were an odd duo. Eric Krull was a young man with dark hair and a slight build. He was hyper-intelligent but intensely socially awkward. He would speak lovingly and at length about each new gadget, and then realize people were paying attention to him and slowly, his volume would decrease and his gaze would wander downward until he appeared to be mumbling to his shoes.

John Johannsen was a bit older – in his mid- to late thirties, by Steven's estimation – but equally awkward, in his own way. He spoke with a slight lisp, and rarely said anything pertinent to the mission or even the technology itself. Instead, he would interject occasional, sarcastic comments about Eric's lack of social skills, or anything else that amused him. He often spoke of his former career as a musician, and seemed to resent the fact that he had joined NASA (and then the organization) rather than sticking with his passion. However, he was quite brilliant in his knowledge of technology, even if he didn't seem very happy about it.

When Larsen had conducted his own search for Carver, he had started by searching for evidence anyplace that Carver had enjoyed going before his downfall. Because Carver had had (had helped invent) devices like the Broom to make traveling the world as effortless as a walk down the block, Larsen's search basically spanned the entirety of Earth. To help narrow it down a bit, Larsen had asked the techs to come up with dronelike devices to scour the earth for traces of Carver. They delivered.

"They're like satellites, almost, but they are intensely powerful and can trace specific molecules, energy signatures, and magical discharges ANYWHERE on the planet!" Eric had said excitedly, when explaining the devices to Steven. "And they're ALL set to find Carver. They are seeking HIS molecules, HIS energy signatures, and his alone. We're gonna track him down, for sure."

John had added, "We were calling them the 'Eyes of Sauron,' but we've shortened it to the 'Eyes' for convenience."

They pulled up the data the Eyes had retrieved. It seemed there had been no strong evidence of Carver's energy traces for two months, when they were picked up in a small town in New Jersey. Steven and Eric both sagged a bit in disappointment; John looked vaguely amused; General Larsen appeared totally unruffled. He clapped Steven on the shoulder.

"Buck up, Drisbane! That's a lot more focused then my search was," the General said, almost jovially. "Off you go to New Jersey. We'll track him down if we have to search under every brick of that town."

That is almost exactly what Steven did, over the course of the next year. He searched every inch of Woodford, New Jersey, meticulously and invisibly. Occasionally, the Eyes would return data that indicated Carver had been somewhere else, and he would travel there, and begin his search again. However, the Eyes picked up residual evidence of Carver in Woodford with some regularity. They were convinced that would be the place to find him; however, he found absolutely no hard evidence, in Woodford or anywhere else. He was beginning to feel rather defeated, and he questioned whether the Eyes were truly a valid tool to go by.

He was enjoying the quiet yet energetic little town of Woodford, though, which he invisibly inhabited while he hunted for Carver.

He liked the quiet, residential neighborhoods full of Victorian homes, and the hustle and bustle of the main street. He liked the quirky characters he saw on Main Street every day. It seemed like a nice place; he often thought he would like to visit again once he was off this assignment.

He messaged Larsen religiously of his progress, or lack thereof. One day, he reported finding a black sock that had been discarded in the street. Though he had no evidence linking it to Carver, he proposed that it could be Carver's sock, based solely on the circumstantial evidence that it was black, as Carver's uniform had been, and in Woodford. He asked to bring it back to the techs for testing.

Larsen apparently did not see the logic of this, as he responded, "Leave it 'til tomorrow. Take the day off. You need a rest."

Steven considered the wisdom of that statement, and decided the General was right. He took a nap for a couple of hours, and then wandered invisibly around town. He had noticed the library from the outside and thought the architecture was impressive; he decided to check it out. It had been a long time since he had enough free time to read for pleasure.

He searched through the fiction section, wondering how long it had been since he had done such a thing. At first, he didn't notice the woman in the aisle. He had become so used to being invisible that he barely registered the presence of civilians anymore. When he bumped into her and she reacted, though, he panicked. There was no way she should be able to see him, much less touch him. He thought she HAD to be working with Carver, there was no other explanation. He went on the offensive.

He treated her as if she were an enemy that needed to be subdued and questioned, and had no qualms about doing so. Her eyes, however, gave him some misgivings. There was fear in her eyes when he had his hand around her neck; there was abject terror in her eyes when the librarian walked through him. He realized she truly had no idea what was happening, and no idea what he was.

"What the hell is happening?" she whispered.

"I was hoping you could tell me. I guess we should talk," he said, squatting so he wouldn't be towering over her. "Are you okay?"

"No." She said it so quietly he barely heard her.

"Fair enough. I'm sorry I choked you. I thought you were.... Someone else," he said lamely. She stared blankly at him, and the librarian came rushing back over and threw an arm around the woman's shoulder.

"It's okay, honey, they're on their way. You're very pale; I don't know what to do. What are you feeling?" the librarian asked the woman.

"Honestly... I don't know," the woman said in a voice so low it was almost a whisper. She spoke to the librarian but she was staring at Steven. "I think I'm seeing things."

"I'm real," Steven said, helpfully. "It's just that no one else can see me. Or hear me. Or touch me.... Or anything me, really. I'm not sure why you can."

"And hearing things," the woman murmured.

"Look at me, Deanna, look at me," the librarian said, grabbing the woman's face in her hands and jerking it toward her so that the woman looked at her eyes. "Your eyes look funny, and you're a little clammy. I think you're going into some kind of shock, Deanna. Do you understand? Do you hear me?"

"Uh-huh," Deanna mumbled, her eyes wandering back to Steven.

"Deanna, huh? That's a pretty name," Steven said.

Deanna's eyes rolled back in her head and she fainted, moments before the ambulance arrived. Steven decided to ride along; he didn't want to lose the strange woman before figuring out why she could see him despite the SmartWand's cloaking settings. Also, he was feeling vaguely guilty about the whole thing for some reason.

"It wasn't really my fault," he thought. Nonetheless, he climbed onto the ambulance, unseen by the EMT's, and rode to the hospital with her.

Deanna

Deanna opened her eyes, disoriented. There was a man in a blue jacket over her, saying, "Talk to me, hon. You with me? You take anything?"

She tried to answer him but there was an oxygen mask over her mouth, so she just shook her head. She felt like they were moving. The last thing she remembered was thinking her heart should not, could not, beat as fast as it was beating… at the library. Yes, she had been at the library. It was all coming back now. The man in black, Barb walking through him, the realization that she was hallucinating. It had been unpleasant.

Feeling very clichéd, she asked the man in the blue jacket, through her oxygen mask, "Where am I?"

"We're going to the hospital, hon, you're gonna be fine. What happened? You sure you didn't take anything?"

"I'm sure," she said drily, wishing she could take the mask off. "I had… some kind of an attack."

"Okay, they'll fix you right up at the hospital. You sure you didn't take anything?"

Another voice, an all-too-familiar voice, said, "For fuck's sake, she didn't take anything." Deanna's eyes widened and she felt her heart start to race again.

The man in the blue jacket, the EMT, continued as if he had heard nothing.

"Cause if you took anything, we need to know so we can help… what happened? You ok?" The EMT checked a band around her arm, checking her blood pressure. "Your blood pressure just skyrocketed. What did you take?"

"Tell him you smoked crack in the library," the man in black said, leaning over the EMT's shoulder. "I just wanna see what he says."

Deanna started hyperventilating, even with the oxygen mask blowing into her mouth and nose. The EMT was frantic as they pulled into the hospital's ambulance-unloading area, turning dials on the oxygen tank and trying desperately to figure out why she was hyperventilating and why her blood pressure had so suddenly escalated. The driver got out and opened the back doors of the van; the two men unloaded the stretcher Deanna was on, popped the wheels down, and rolled her into the emergency room. A woman in a white coat, wearing a stethoscope around her neck and carrying a clipboard, rushed to greet them.

41

"What's the situation?" the woman asked.

"Not sure, we got a call from the library, where the woman was unconscious. Librarian said she had some kind of attack, and then fainted. She – the librarian - thought the patient went into some kind of shock. The patient came to on the ride over, seemed ok, but then her blood pressure went from 120/70 to 150/100 within seconds, and she started hyperventilating under the mask," the EMT responded.

The man in black, standing behind them, said, "Well, that's not good. You really need to calm down."

Deanna was fairly certain her heart was going to explode, it was beating so fast. She was petrified, both because she was seeing and hearing a person no one else heard or saw – a person other people could walk through – and because she feared being locked in the psych ward. It was one of her greatest fears, to wind up like that. Her trip to the adolescent unit the psychiatric hospital twenty years earlier had been bad enough. The idea of winding up as an adult locked away in a straightjacket, a permanent source of heartbreak for her parents with no control over her own existence, at the mercy of doctors....it terrified her. So, she stayed quiet.

She was wheeled into a tiny room, where the doctors removed her shirt and stuck suction cups with wires around them to her chest, presumably to monitor her heart rate and vitals. She was embarrassed to be sitting on a cot in just her bra in front of the man in black, then mad at herself for being embarrassed about a hallucination seeing her without her shirt.

Someone put a hospital gown over her torso, and she was grateful.

They swapped out her ambulance oxygen mask, which the EMT's took, for another oxygen mask.

The woman in white said, "You didn't take anything, did you? Any pills or coke or anything? We can't help you unless you tell us."

The man in black said, "Seriously, do they want you to be on drugs? Do they not have any other illnesses around here?"

Deanna shook her head, and murmured, "Nothing, no drugs."

The woman in white said, "Okay, I'm gonna give you something to bring your heart rate down. You're gonna feel a little pinch." A needle stabbed her in the arm, and released something that stung a bit under her skin as it came out of the needle.

"So if you're not on drugs, they're gonna put you on drugs," the man in black said. "That's an awesome system."

Deanna was quickly learning to tune him out. She was feeling calmer by the second, too. Whatever the stinging substance in the needle had been, it was a-ok in her book. Everything was going to be fine, she decided.

The woman in the white coat watched a screen over Deanna's head for a few minutes, and then adjusted her oxygen mask. "Your heart rate's looking pretty good, now. We're gonna let you rest for a couple minutes, and then take some blood tests, okay? We'll figure out what's going on, don't worry."

Deanna nodded. Rest sounded good. "It's really cold in here," she said aloud.

The other woman pulled a thin blanket over her, and then left the room. Deanna heard machines beeping and feet walking by the door every few seconds, but it was white noise. Her eyelids were drooping.

"We really do need to talk," the man in black said.

"Nope," Deanna whispered. "You're not even a person."

"Look... Deanna... I am a real person, I promise. You're just gonna have to accept the fact that I am real but no one else can see me, and we'll talk more once we're out of here."

She shook her head slightly.

"We can talk here, but people are gonna think you're talking to yourself. I'm trying to protect you, here, not me."

Deanna shrugged a shoulder.

"You're an incredibly frustrating woman, do you know that?"

"You're an incredibly annoying hallucination, do you know that?" Deanna replied, though slightly muffled through the oxygen mask.

"Look, Deanna," he grabbed her chin gently and tilted her face upward, staring into her eyes. "I am not a hallucination. I am real. My name is Steven. No one else can see me because... because I am disguised by magic," he said. "But you can see me, and you can hear me and feel me, so please just trust your senses and understand that I am real."

She stared up at him, remembering the Charles DeLint quote that had crossed her mind earlier: "That's the thing about magic: You have to know that it's here, it's all around us, or it just stays invisible to you." She had always wanted so badly for that to be true, for magic to be manifesting all around her, unseen by eyes that had become jaded by society and experience. Could it really be true? Magic? Her mind reeled.

Aloud, she said, "Disguised by... magic."

He nodded.

"Are you a ghost?"

He chuckled. "I am alive and well, though calling me a spook would not be totally off base."

"Like... a CIA kind of spook?"

He shook his head. "Not CIA, no. I work for a different outfit. You haven't heard of us."

"What kind of work do you do?"

"You ask a lot of questions," he said, smiling slightly.

"There's an invisible man talking to me in a hospital bed. I have some questions."

Steven quirked an eyebrow. "Fair enough," he said, finally taking his hand away from her face and sitting back a bit. "Do you wanna get out of here?"

Deanna blinked. "I mean... can I?"

He nodded and pulled out his phone again, tapping away at the touch screen. Deanna cocked her head, confused. "What are you, texting your ride?"

The corner of Steven's mouth lifted in a half smile, his eyes never leaving the screen. "It's not a phone. I'm just... changing a couple of things." He paused, glanced over at her. "How are you feeling now?"

She took stock of herself, and realized she was absolutely fine. Better than fine, she felt great. Her heart was beating normally, her breathing was fine... come to think of it, she had more energy than she had had in a while. That feeling of wanting to hibernate that plagued her all winter, and the sleepy effects of whatever the doctor had given her, were gone.

"I feel great," she said, and he nodded, turning back to his not-phone. "What did you do?"

"I told you, I'm just changing a couple of things."

"What is that thing?" Deanna nodded toward the not-phone.

"Long story. Where do you live?"

Deanna told him her address and he said, "Got it." He continued typing for a few minutes, then pulled another device out of his pocket. It was a little round black thing. She stared at it, wondering what it was, while he pushed a button and...

They were sitting on the couch in her living room.

"What the hell?" she said, looking around. She did not feel nearly as disoriented as she felt she should after experiencing such a sudden change. Had she not been holding on to the memory of being in the hospital, she would have thought they'd been on the couch the entire time they were having this discussion. It felt very natural.

44

"It's just molecular changes and stuff...." Steven said vaguely, waving a hand slightly. She continued staring at him, so he added, "More magic."

She nodded. That seemed obvious, at least. "I didn't even notice we were moving or anything."

"It was a relatively short distance. Longer distances cause a slight feeling of vertigo."

She nodded again, amazed. "So.....how'd you do that?"

"Years of training," he said shortly, successfully avoiding the question. "So, who are you, Deanna? Why can you see me?"

She shrugged, shaking her head. "I'm nobody. I'm a waitress... actually, I'm not even that anymore. I don't know..." She thought for a bit. "I've always wanted magic to be real. I always hoped it was real. Could that be it?"

He stared at her. "Maybe," he assented. "I don't really see how, but the energy is definitely very reactive to belief. There's got to be more than that, though."

"The energy?"

"Magic," he said. "I think we're going to have to do some tests."

Her eyebrows furrowed. "Like, magic tests?"

"I guess you could say that."

"How? What kind of tests?"

"Well, I've already scanned you with everything I've got and come up blank. I think I'm gonna have to bring you in," Steven said casually, apparently not realizing how ominous this sounded to her.

"Bring me in WHERE?"

"To my... to my boss. I've never experienced anything like this before. We're going to need some help figuring it out."

"Your boss? Who's your boss?"

Steven smiled. "He's going to like you, actually. He likes when people ask questions." He started tapping away on his not-phone again, saying, "I'm just briefing him now."

"You said that thing wasn't a phone."

"It's not," he said, with that satisfied little half-smile again. "They're ready for us."

"Wait," Deanna said, panicking. "I'm really not okay with going to some mysterious place where people are going to run tests on me."

Steven nodded and shrugged a shoulder, while continuing to tap on his device. "I get that. But the thing is – "

Deanna felt a sudden feeling of vertigo.

"The thing is," Steven continued, "you don't really have a choice."

The feeling of vertigo dissipated, and Deanna's head felt clearer. However, something felt wrong. It took her a moment to realize they were no longer in her living room. She was sitting in exactly the same position she had been in on her couch, but the chair underneath her was a comparatively uncomfortable metallic affair. The room they were in was small, with dark grey walls, a dark grey carpet, and a dark grey ceiling; it was terribly gloomy, she thought. Steven, rather than sitting a few feet away on her couch, was now seated in a chair identical to her own, on the other side of a small table which was immediately next to her.

After taking a moment to assess her surroundings, Deanna felt a vague sense of anxiety that was almost immediately pushed aside by an overwhelming rush of pure rage. The sense of awe and wonder that Steven had awakened in her by showing her that magic was real dissipated in the face of her current situation. She found herself in a completely unfamiliar place, with no idea where she was or how far from home, and she had no control over when or even whether she could return home. She felt frightened and helpless, and feeling like that – like a victim – made her angry.

She stood and faced him with fire in her eyes. "You're a complete bastard."

Steven made the fatal mistake of uttering a chuckle; he actually said, "Ha!" It was a surprised reaction, but Deanna did not take it that way.

"You kidnapped me, you absolute prick," she snarled.

Steven also stood up, looking down at her, and she noticed that his eyes were a colder, paler blue than she had previously thought.

"I brought you here to help you as much as anyone else," he said quietly but icily. "I would advise you to watch your tone."

"Would you? I guess it's lucky for me I don't take advice from kidnappers."

"You're being ridiculous. I did not kidnap you. We are facing a confusing situation – we are BOTH facing a confusing situation – and I brought you here so we can get to the bottom of it. I'm sorry if you feel inconvenienced, but you have to think of the greater good, here."

"Inconvenienced? You just whisked me away from my home and anything that is familiar to me, to some dark, gloomy place I've never been, and I don't even know where I am! That's more than just an 'inconvenience.' You essentially just stole my freedom, and I have no idea what your intentions are."

Steven's tone softened slightly, though his facial expression remained hostile. "I didn't mean to scare you. You will not be harmed while you are here. But we NEED to find out why all of the shielding that makes me undetectable to literally everyone else has no effect on you."

"But...." Deanna trailed off, looking away for a moment. "I don't want to be trapped like some kind of a lab rat."

A new voice, behind her, said, "I assure you, young lady, you are neither trapped nor shall you be treated like any kind of a rat."

She whirled around, surprised. A short, stocky man with grey hair and wire rimmed glasses stood behind her. Like Steven, he wore all black. She did not know when he had entered the room or how much of the conversation he had heard; she assumed he had arrived by the same magical means that Steven had used to bring her here. (This assumption would turn out to be correct.)

"Who are you?"

The man smiled convivially and offered his hand, which Deanna shook awkwardly as he introduced himself. "They call me General Larsen, around here, but you can call me Benjamin. Drisbane tells me you are completely immune to his shields and that is fascinating to me, absolutely fascinating. I really can't tell you how intrigued I am by you."

"Drisbane?" Deanna asked bemusedly.

"Me. Steven Drisbane," Steven said, while Larsen said, "Oh, perhaps he didn't introduce himself properly. The young man who brought you here is Ensign Steven Drisbane." The general stopped speaking and peered around the room as if looking for something. "Are you here, Drisbane?"

"Oh, right," Steven said, pulling out his phone-like device and tapping away at the screen. A moment or two later, the General's gaze went directly to him for the first time and the older man smiled again.

"It's good to see you, Ensign."

"It's good to be seen, sir."

Deanna looked back and forth between the two men. "You really didn't know he was there?" she asked Larsen.

"I'm afraid not, my dear. Your ability to see through the Wand's shielding abilities truly is unique."

"The Wand?"

"This," Steven said, holding up his not-phone.

"Not exactly how one pictures a magic wand," Deanna murmured. She blinked and shook her head, trying to clear away some of her confusion. "You're an ensign?" she addressed Steven. "Like on Star Trek?"

He gave her that half smile again, an expression she was beginning to loathe. He looked so arrogant and smug. "More like in the Navy," he said.

"You guys are in the Navy?"

"No," Larsen answered smoothly. "Now tell me, my dear, what is your name?"

Though she was beginning to feel as if she had fallen down the rabbit hole, Deanna answered calmly and cordially. "I'm Deanna. Deanna Flanagan. May I ask why I am here, exactly?"

"Of course you may, Ms. Flanagan, and may I say that is a lovely name," Larsen answered, his eyes twinkling. "Your ability to see through our shields is simply extraordinary, and we would like to run some tests to try and find the cause of your ability."

"What kind of tests?"

"Nothing too invasive, I assure you. Mostly, we will just wave some devices at you and look at our computers."

Deanna thought for a moment before posing her next question. "Without putting too fine a point on it, what's in it for me? What if I just want to go home? Will you let me go?"

Larsen offered a wide, magnanimous smile. "My dear, I would imagine you are as eager to find the cause of your abilities as we are! Drisbane has shared with me that you have long believed in magic. Imagine if you have some access to it! Think of how much you can learn from us."

Noting that he had quite artfully avoided answering her questions, Deanna tried another line of inquiry. "I don't know what I can learn from you because I don't know anything about you. What kind of a place is this? Who do you two work for? What do you do, exactly?"

"We're the good guys," Steven said quietly. She glanced at him and saw a kind of earnest pride shining through his eyes.

"Well said, Drisbane. Ms. Flanagan, there is no need to be afraid," Larsen said in a gentle tone. "We are part of an organization exclusively dedicated to the study and use of magic. We use it to protect our great nation and generally improve the world at large. It is our mission to eliminate needless suffering of any kind, and we hope to do that through developing a greater understanding of and control over the energy you know as magic."

"I often think of us as students," Steven interjected.

"Precisely, Ensign. We are students of magic, students of the mysteries of the universe, and you, Ms. Flanagan, seem to be one of those mysteries."

Deanna mulled this over for a moment. She had a strong suspicion that the men would not allow her to leave. A sense of unease and fear slithered around in her belly. However, she was definitely curious to learn more about magic. The range of emotions she was experiencing was vast and overwhelming.

"After... after you run these tests on me," she stammered, "will you... will I be allowed to go home?"

"I give you my word, Ms. Flanagan, that we will not keep you here a moment longer than necessary."

She nodded, though his statement made her feel no more at ease. She didn't really feel like she had a choice, though, so she decided to make the best of it. The sooner they did whatever they needed to do, the sooner she could go home.

Looking up at the General, she said, "I guess.... I guess we should get started."

Steven

Steven was frustrated.

For several hours, he, Larsen, Eric, and John had been scanning Deanna with every device in their arsenal. They examined every molecule of her being, and found no abnormalities. The energy signature she emitted was similarly unremarkable. Larsen had interviewed her endlessly, but could find no patterns or even unexplained series of coincidences in her life which he felt could lead to understanding her immunity to magical shields. Every attempt they made to figure out what made Deanna unique lead to the same conclusion: she was a normal, average human being.

Steven was tired, hungry, and generally frustrated by the lack of progress they had made. Every second he spent unsuccessfully trying to solve the puzzle of Deanna was a second he could be spending tracking Carver. The fact that his search for Carver had also been so far unsuccessful made today's lack of progress that much more vexing; Steven was beginning to feel as if nothing were working for him.

He stood, pushing his chair back, and everyone looked at him. "General," he addressed Larsen, "May I have a word with you?"

"Of course, Drisbane," Larsen replied, sounding tired. "I could use a break, anyway. Let's go grab a cup of coffee."

The two men left the room as Eric and John decided to re-scan Deanna's energy output. Steven was glad to leave, rather than repeat the same exercises in futility they had engaged in all day.

"So what's on your mind?" the General asked as they strolled down the hall.

"Well, sir... I'm just so damn frustrated," Steven blurted. "I haven't found Carver, and now I ran into this woman who is totally immune to our magical shields, and we don't know why. I feel like we need to know why, but I don't know how to find out. The whole thing is taking time away from my mission, which, again, has yielded no real results. I'm starting to feel like a dog chasing its own tail."

"I understand, Drisbane. I've had similar feelings, myself, regarding Carver." Larsen paused as they entered a small kitchenette, where he smelled the coffee in the pot on the burner, made a face, and dumped it. As he set about brewing a new pot, he continued, "I am actually wondering if Ms. Flanagan is a new lead."

Steven paused. "I'm confused."

"I think it's safe to say we all are, at the moment."

"I mean… what do *you* mean? How could she be a new lead?"

"Well," the General mused, "you found her while on the search for Carver. In the same town where Carver's energy signature has been appearing on an intermittent but recurring basis for over a year now. Perhaps there is some connection. Perhaps there is even something unusual about the place itself. As you know, coincidence is rarely just coincidence. It generally means something bigger."

Steven thought about it for a moment, then shook his head. "I just don't see it. I don't understand how an out-of-work waitress could lead us to Carver."

"Maybe it's a line of questioning we need to start, and we'll see where it leads," Larsen replied. "What's that expression? You don't have to be able to see the top of the staircase to take the first step? Something like that. Point is, we won't know the answers until we start asking the questions, so let's start asking the woman if she knows David Carver."

Steven shrugged and nodded his assent, then poured himself a cup of freshly brewed coffee. "I suppose you're right, sir."

Moments later, the two men re-entered the little lab where Deanna sat between Eric and John, each on their computers. The two techs spoke to each other (and, in Eric's case, sometimes to himself) as if she were an inanimate object, unable to hear them.

"She's definitely not emanating anything special," John said. "Just as dull as dull can be."

Deanna stared blankly at him. Very purposefully blankly.

"I'm gonna try the atomic phase scan again," Eric murmured. "We could be missing some anomaly on the atomic level."

"We've already run it twice, numbnuts," John snapped. "Nothing."

"Gentlemen," Larsen interrupted. "Perhaps you should take a short break, grab a cup of coffee and regroup. I would like the opportunity to speak with Ms. Flanagan."

"Fine by me. This is boring," John said, and the two men left the room. Deanna stared quietly and expectantly at the General from her chair.

"Ms. Flanagan," he began. "Have you ever met a man by the name of David Carver?"

She furrowed her brow for a moment. "Not that I know of."

"A fair point, perhaps you encountered him without catching his name. Here," Larsen tapped on his Wand and pulled up a picture of

Carver, the same one he had shown Steven during their first meeting. It showed Carver a couple of years before his desertion, looking happy, healthy, and quite sane.

Deanna studied the picture for a second, then shook her head and shrugged.

"He'd be older now," Steven interjected. "Try to picture him about twenty years older than he is there."

She stared at the picture again, looking no less confused. "I'm sorry, I don't know that person. Should I?"

Larsen stared penetratingly at her for several long seconds. "I'm not sure. I have a bit of a hypothesis that somehow, you two are connected."

"Does he see through your magic shields, too?"

"Not exactly." Larsen did not offer further explanation.

"We don't know what he looks like, exactly, now. He may have changed a lot since that picture was taken," Steven offered. "He's been going through a rough time for the better part of two decades, now. His eyes, I can tell you, look different."

Deanna's brow furrowed as she studied the picture. "Different how?"

Steven pictured Carver as he had looked all those years earlier, on his motorcycle. "Darker. Scarier. Kind of … haunted."

She narrowed her eyes, looking as if she were trying to remember something. Steven and Larsen stayed quiet, giving her time to think. After a moment, she muttered, "It couldn't be."

"What?" Steven nearly barked at her. "It couldn't be what?"

"There was this homeless guy in Woodford last summer. We called him the Rasta Man because he had this one long, filthy dreadlock. He was really, really thin, and he looked really frail. Much smaller than the guy in the picture, and dirtier. And he had these crazy, dark eyes. They looked haunted, like you said. They were kind of frightening."

"Where is he now?" Larsen asked, doing a much better job than Steven had at keeping his voice calm and level.

"I don't know, he kind of disappeared when it got colder. I assumed he found someplace to stay, because of winter. He just wandered around in the summer. I don't know where he slept."

Steven decided to stay quiet and let Larsen do the questioning; the General had a special talent for putting people at ease and figuring out the truth behind their words.

"Tell me more about him," he began. "Did you speak with this Rasta Man?"

"Kind of," Deanna responded. "He was very difficult to understand. He sort of just jabbered random syllables, not real words. He would throw in sentence fragments here and there, but often it made no sense."

"Tell me some of the things he said that made no sense."

"Well, he would bum cigarettes off me sometimes. He would kind of talk, some of those times. Other times he'd just point at my cigarette. Like I said, his words were mostly gibberish. The couple of things I recall were totally random, like when he said he never ate a day in his life. Actually, I was just recently remembering the last time I saw him. He said more that day than I had ever heard out of him. He said he had had a brand new motorcycle once, but he wasn't sure where he left it. 'Maybe Ohio,' he said."

Steven felt his knee start twitching involuntarily from the excitement he felt. The comment about the motorcycle made him believe that Deanna's Rasta Man truly was Carver. This was the closest he'd gotten to accomplishing his mission in months. This was much better than finding a cast-off black sock in the street. This woman had actually seen Carver, spoken with him; she might provide the clue that would bring Steven to Carver.

"When was that? The last time you saw him?" he asked, trying to keep his voice level.

"Last August, I think?"

"Let's back up," Larsen instructed. "When was the first time you saw him?"

"Well," Deanna mused. "I noticed him around for a few months before he ever spoke to me. He would often wander around on Main Street, or just squat in the middle of the sidewalk, talking to himself. He was rather off-putting. Most people gave him a wide berth. I know I did, to start."

"And when was that, when you first noticed him around?"

"Spring? Maybe March or April of last year?"

"You said it took him a few months to talk to you. So he approached you in roughly May?"

"Yeah, around then. He wanted a cigarette. He made that clear by pointing at the one I was smoking. I didn't understand a word he said, that day. He scared me a bit."

53

Steven stood quietly and observed as Larsen continued questioning Deanna for the better part of an hour. She had no hard evidence indicating that the Rasta Man was actually Carver, but it was the best lead they'd had in a long time, and they wanted to know every detail of her encounters with him.

Eric and John returned to the room while they spoke, and observed the conversation. Eric took on the task of reviewing all of the readings they had which had sent Steven to Woodford to begin with.

Once Deanna had explained each minor conversation she had had with the Rasta Man at least three times over, there was silence in the room for several long minutes.

Finally, Steven asked Eric, "Anything she said help interpret our readings?"

"The timeline adds up. His energy signatures were in that area at the end of last summer, and have been there sporadically ever since."

There was another moment of silence as all four men considered possibilities. Deanna finally interrupted the silence by stammering, "Does this...did it....does this help? Are we done? Can I go home?"

Larsen glanced at her and said, "Not just yet, my dear. But we have made some considerable progress, I think. Let's all get some rest and reconvene here in a few hours. Drisbane, show Ms. Flanagan to the guest quarters."

Steven nodded and gestured toward the hallway, so Deanna stood and followed him. They walked down the hallway in silence as he mulled over the idea of the legendary, once-brilliant Carver living as a homeless, crazy wanderer.

"Can I ask you a question?" Deanna asked, jarring him from his reverie. He nodded.

"Why is this David Carver guy so important to you people?" She drew to halt and stared at him with her wide, green eyes, awaiting a response. He was momentarily taken aback. She had become, in his mind, a subject; someone to be questioned, tested. He was not expecting such a question from her.

"Ah. Well," he began clumsily. "That's sort of ... classified."

"How, precisely, can something be 'sort of' classified?"

"It's classified. You just caught me off guard," he admitted.

"It would seem that I've been helpful to some kind of search you have going for this man. Doesn't that put me in a position to know what I've helped with?"

"Ah…" Steven faltered. He couldn't think of an answer that would satisfy her and make her stop asking questions. However, he was unwilling to tell her the truth without first discussing it with the General. "I think you should ask General Larsen these kind of questions. It would be his decision how much you should know."

"I see," Deanna said softly. She looked up at him for a moment, then continued, "I asked you because I think your General Larsen is a little too good at being evasive."

Steven didn't know what to say, so he turned and continued walking down the hall. He reached a door that looked exactly like all the other doors, and swung it open, gesturing for Deanna to enter.

"These will be your quarters," he said, expressionlessly. "The bathroom is over there. We've already filled the cabinets with toiletries, pajamas, and a change of clothes. I will be back to get you in the morning. If you need anything else, you can let me know then."

"Back to 'get' me?" Deanna narrowed her eyes. "Couldn't I just meet you in the testing room?"

He hesitated for a split second before saying, "It's too easy to get lost, here. Good night."

Then he shut the door before she could ask any more questions. He was a bit out of practice at dealing with civilians, and it was getting too difficult to avoid answering her. He would have to consult with the General to find out how to respond to her.

Deanna

Deanna tried the handle seconds after Steven shut her into the room, and was totally unsurprised to find she was locked in. The fact that she had seen it coming made it no less frustrating or anxiety-inducing for her. She decided to go with feeling frustrated, as it was less scary, so she punched the door.

It hurt rather badly.

The door felt like it was made of iron, though it appeared to be an ordinary, wooden door. She had been expecting a satisfying "thud" sound, which would hopefully echo through the hall and let Steven or whoever else might be within earshot know that she was angry, and not at all scared. Instead, there was a complete lack of sound, as if she had just punched a wall of cotton.

She stood, staring at the door and sucking on her freshly injured knuckles.

Her burgeoning anxiety, seeing that frustration had done more harm than good, decided to take over. Her heart fluttered unpleasantly in her chest.

As she tried to clear her mind and maintain calm, she let her gaze wander around the small room. It looked terribly institutional. There was a small, twin-sized bed with a thin, uncomfortable-looking mattress covered with thin, grey sheets and blankets. A nondescript grey dresser stood against the grey wall. As a test, she opened a drawer. In the drawer were two pairs of grey cotton-poly blend pants with elastic waistbands. She opened another drawer and found large, shapeless t-shirts to match.

"Pajamas and a change of clothes," she murmured as she recalled Steven's words, noting how the clothes resembled a prison uniform.

She walked into bathroom, and was totally unsurprised that it was done in grey tile, with a grey sink, and a grey toilet seat. She wondered if they had chosen to color everything grey in order to depress all who entered this building. If so, it was working. She felt rather hopeless.... Lost, trapped, and hopeless.

After attempting to distract herself from her thoughts by performing ordinary rituals like brushing her teeth and washing her face, she decided to take advantage of her solitude by meditating. In her real life, before she had fallen down the metaphorical rabbit hole of meeting Steven that day, meditation had become a helpful activity (or rather, lack of activity) during her months of fruitlessly searching for a job. It helped her feel calm and clear headed, rather than distraught and full of doubt.

Though being held prisoner by some kind of secret military organization with magic at their disposal seemed a little harder to deal with than looking for a job, she hoped meditation would bring her some peace.

Sitting on the bed with her legs crossed, she closed her eyes and tried to clear her mind.

"I'm being held prisoner by a secret military organization," her mind screamed.

"Shhhhhh, be clear, mind," she thought, with equal intensity.

After waging this fruitless battle against her own thoughts for a few minutes, she remembered something she had read in books by Wayne Dyer, Deepak Chopra, Louise Hay, and other teachers of metaphysical well-being: when one is meditating and thoughts enter the mind, one should not resist the thoughts. Instead, one should acknowledge the thought and lovingly, gratefully release it.

So, she switched tactics. As every thought entered her mind, she acknowledged it and released it with as much love and gratitude as she could muster.

"I'm a prisoner," she thought. "Thanks for that, thought, 'bye now," she answered herself.

"This really sucks," came another thought. "Indeed. I release you now, thought."

"Damn it," she thought. "I left my clothes at the dryer in the laundromat before I went to the library."

"And that's okay, I will ask the military guys to help me get it tomorrow. They can transport people for miles in the blink of an eye, I'm sure they can rescue a load of forgotten laundry. I release you now, laundry thought, thanks for coming."

On and on it went, as a seemingly endless parade of thoughts entered her mind, and were released, until finally, blessedly, she found herself in a state of inner quiet. Rather than thinking, worrying, and freaking out, she focused on feeling gratitude, and tried to list all the things she was grateful for.

"I'm really grateful to be healthy," she thought, and focused on that feeling. "I'm grateful to be alive, and to have a home to go back to if I ever get out of here. I'm grateful for my parents, and my friends, and all of the love I have experienced in my life."

Putting her focus on all of the good things in her life made her feel quite a bit better. She relaxed so much, in fact, that the next thing she knew, she was dreaming. She knew she was dreaming, and that she must have fallen asleep while meditating, but that knowledge gave her no control over the dream as it unfolded around her.

She was in some sort of great hall. It was an enormous place, with stone walls and floors, and wooden beams overhead. Statues stood all around her; white marble statues, grey stone statues, abstract metal statues… the only thing they seemed to have in common was that they were all statues of humans (although some of the more abstract ones gave her a moment's pause before she figured that out). Most of them were worn down by the passage of time; some were broken, missing limbs or noses or even a head.

For some time, nothing happened; there was no movement in the cavernous chamber of her dream. She simply wandered around, idly observing the statues. Silence and stillness permeated the chamber and into the very core of her being. Then, suddenly, parts of each statue began to detach and float toward one statue that stood in the center of the room. This center statue was of a woman, and it was one of the ones that had somehow, over time, lost its head.

As Deanna watched, various arms, legs, torsos, and heads detached from other statues and floated toward the headless woman. Some of the pieces attached themselves to her in seemingly random positions; an arm affixed itself to her back, a leg to her abdomen. It seemed odd to Deanna, in her dream state, that none of the pieces landed on the top of the statue's neck, where her head would be had she not lost it. Other pieces landed on the floor around the statue, leaning in the headless woman's direction as if giving her audience.

All of this happened in just a few seconds. Once all of the fragments of other statues were apparently satisfied with their positions around the statue of the headless woman, stillness once again reigned in the hall. Deanna realized she was holding her breath, and she exhaled slowly. As she did so, a bright, glowing orb appeared above the tableau, right where the center statue's head would have been. It was like a tiny sun. Even in her dream, Deanna had to shield her eyes from its brightness.

After it shone for a few seconds, music began to play. It seemed to come from everywhere and nowhere at the same time, as if an entire orchestra was all around her and playing for all they were worth while simultaneously being invisible. The pieces that had so recently attached themselves to and surrounded the statue now detached and floated a short distance away. As they landed, they joined together and even grew new appendages. Each one, once a broken piece of statuary, became whole. It was like watching the birth of an art gallery, or possibly the creation of the Universe. Deanna couldn't decide which. She knew only that it was absolutely exquisite to watch, and even more so in the bright light of the tiny sun.

The light began to dim, and Deanna turned her attention back to the headless statue of the woman in time to see the light fading and becoming a head. The process took a moment. Then, that statue, too, was whole, and disturbingly familiar. Deanna stepped closer to it, scrutinizing its new head. She stood directly in front of the statue, examining its features. She realized it bore quite a bit of resemblance to the face she saw each day in the mirror, and smiled to herself at the notion of a statue of Deanna. She had an arbitrary desire to touch the statue's face, and her hand floated up to do so. She felt very detached, almost disembodied, as she watched her hand drift closer to the statue's white marble face and her fingers caress the marble.

Suddenly, the statue's eyes snapped open and the mouth smiled at her. Although its countenance could only be described as joyful, the sudden movement startled Deanna. Her own sudden intake of breath forced her into waking.

For a second, she had no idea where she was. Then, she remembered: the organization, the locked door, the tiny bed in her "quarters."

"Well, no wonder I'm having weird dreams," she thought. "I'm having a pretty freaking weird day."

She lay there for what seemed like a very long time, staring at the ceiling and remembering her dream. She didn't feel like she could fall back to sleep, but she was locked in the room and had nowhere to go. She desperately wanted a cigarette, but had none on her and imagined that even if she did, lighting one would probably set off some fire alarms or even sprinklers in this institutional setting.

At some point, she must have dozed off. The next thing she knew, she was being startled awake by a hand on her shoulder. She gasped and sat up, causing Steven to take a step back.

He held up a mug in one hand, as if it were some kind of a peace offering. "I brought coffee."

She eyed him warily for a moment, gathering her wits before reaching for the mug. The light was no different in the small, windowless room than it had been when she first went to sleep. It was discombobulating.

"What time is it?" she finally asked, after sipping the coffee. It had a lot more cream and sugar than she would have liked, but beggars can't be choosers, and she did love a hot cup of coffee in the morning.

"Seven. We thought you should sleep in a bit," Steven replied. It took her a second to realize he was serious. Obviously, secret government agencies worked on a different schedule than former restaurant employees.

"Um....thanks," she said with as much sincerity as she could muster through the sleep-addled haze of her mind. "What now?"

"Breakfast. Then we have some more tests."

Breakfast was not what she expected. She had not spent much time picturing what it would be like, on their walk through the empty halls, but when Steven stopped at a door that looked like every other door, she did not expect it to lead to a fairly large, well-lit cafeteria in which twenty or thirty other organization operatives were enjoying their breakfasts. For a second she just stood and stared.

"This is the cafeteria," Steven explained.

"I kind of got that," Deanna answered.

"Well, you looked confused."

"It's just...." Deanna faltered, then rallied. "It's so bright. And I didn't know anyone except you, the General, and those techie guys were here."

"Well, there are quite a few of us," Steven said, as he motioned for her to walk with him to the food line.

The room was about the size of a school cafeteria, with white floors, tables, and chairs. Fluorescent lighting cast its horrifyingly bright illumination down on the black-clad men and women of the organization. Many of them seemed to examine Deanna as she passed. She felt very exposed, and very out of place.

Steven drew to a halt in front of what Deanna had originally mistaken for an ordinary cafeteria food line, and took two black trays off of a pile at the end of the counter. Once Deanna was close enough to look properly at the food line, she realized that there was no food under the glass sneeze guards, nor were there employees waiting to dole out food behind the line. Instead, there were matte black squares around another raised black square under the glass. Steven put his hand on one of the matte black squares, and a plate heaped with eggs and bacon appeared on the raised square.

As he took his plate from the raised square, Steven told her, "You just have to think about what you want for breakfast, believe you can have it, and put your hand on the square."

"I'm not generally a breakfast person," Deanna replied.

Steven looked at her in a way she thought was very condescending as he said, "You need to have breakfast. We have a long day ahead, and I don't know when you'll get another chance to eat."

She looked at him, shrugged, and looked at the squares. She pictured her usual mornings at home and, feeling a bit silly, put her hand on one of the squares.

A pack of Marlboro Lights, a lighter, a cup of coffee, and what appeared to be her cell phone appeared on the raised square. They both stared at it for a brief moment before Deanna reached for her bounty. Steven grabbed her hand, stopping her, and said, "Really?"

"I told you, I'm not a breakfast person," she replied, sweeping up the cigarettes with her other hand. "I usually have a cigarette and coffee and screw around on my phone for a few when I wake up, before I meditate and get started with my day."

He shook his head in disbelief and grabbed the cell phone with his free hand, then released her hand. "I'm afraid you can't use this here. No service, and we don't need to be tracked. But after I eat, I will bring you outside so you can smoke a cigarette. You really do have to eat, though." As he said this, he put his hand on a square and produced a breakfast very similar to his own.

Deanna nearly forgot all of the hostility she had developed toward Steven in her anticipation of a cigarette. "Thank you," she said. "I can't tell you how much I would appreciate that. I've been dying for a cigarette since I got here."

"I used to smoke," he said, with an air of confidence as he walked toward an unoccupied table. "I gave it up when I joined the Navy. Well," he said thoughtfully as he pulled out a chair and sat down, "I still have one every now and again. Mostly if I'm drinking. Not that I've had a chance to do that for over a year now."

"Why?" Deanna asked.

"I've been on assignment," he replied.

"Looking for this David Carver guy?"

Steven's spine straightened and he looked tense for a moment, then gave a perfunctory nod. He shoveled food into his mouth; Deanna assumed he was trying to avoid further conversation. She felt like she was learning more about her captors by the second, though. She now knew that Steven, at least, was in the Navy, even though Larsen had said the day before that they were not. She wasn't sure if that information was important, but at least she had learned something.

Excited by the possibility of an imminent cigarette, she dug into her breakfast.

Steven

Steven was finding Deanna remarkably easy to talk to. Almost too easy; he wasn't sure he should have admitted he had been on assignment looking for Carver. He had not yet conferred with Larsen to ascertain what he was or was not allowed to tell her. It had been a long time since he had been in casual conversation with a woman, though, and he realized his guard was down. He filled his mouth with food to prevent himself from blurting anything else out without thinking.

As he chewed, he looked Deanna over. For the first time, he was looking at her as a woman rather than a test subject. He had to admit, she was really pretty.

"So tell me about yourself, Deanna," he said lightly after he watched her eat for long enough that he was starting to feel awkward. "What do you do when you're not hanging out in libraries and violating laws of magic?"

She studied his face for a second, as if she were trying to figure something out, before answering, "Little of this, little of that."

"There were a lot of paintings in your apartment. Do you paint?"

She shrugged a shoulder and said, "I dabble."

"How long have you been living in Woodford?"

"A while," she answered. Steven was beginning to realize she wasn't going to be very forthcoming with information, so he finished his breakfast in silence. He was kind of surprised to realize that he really wanted to find a way to put her at ease. He wasn't sure why he cared. He figured it was because he had found her and brought her here, almost as if she was a stray cat he had become responsible for.

As she finished her last bite, he said, "Come on, let's get you your cigarette." The smile she flashed warmed his heart. He found that he, too, was smiling as they left the cafeteria and strolled down the hall.

As they approached the exit, he had a sudden urge to give her his jacket. He proffered the black pea coat and said, "It's cold out, wear this."

She looked at him strangely and said, "Thanks," as she put it on. He wondered what she was thinking.

Once outside, he watched with amusement as she lit her cigarette and inhaled it deeply, closing her eyes in pleasure as she did so. When she exhaled, she nearly moaned, "Dear God, I needed this."

Feeling genuinely relieved by her pleasure, Steven decided it was a good time to make conversation. "You really should think about quitting, you know."

She shot him a look that made him rethink the idea of conversation, so he just quietly watched her smoke. After a few drags, she asked, "What are you guys going to do to me today?"

"I actually haven't been briefed yet," he explained, "but I imagine it will be very much like yesterday."

She nodded, and finished her cigarette in silence. Hours later, as Steven watched the General interrogating Deanna on his Wand, he would remember that moment and realize how incredibly wrong he had been.

He realized something was different when they walked into the testing room, but it took him a moment to realize what it was. One wall of the room had been transformed into a pane of glass. On the other side of the glass, there was a new, tiny room in which the only furniture was a very small, uncomfortable looking chair under a hanging lamp.

"Drisbane. Bring the subject in there," the general said by way of greeting, gesturing toward the room on the other side of the glass. He did not even glance at Deanna.

Steven opened the glass door and ushered Deanna in, noting the fear in her eyes and giving her what he hoped was an encouraging smile. "Don't worry," he whispered before he shut the door. "You're going to be fine."

She did not look convinced.

Once he shut the door, Steven turned to his commanding officer and said, "Can she hear us?"

"No. Can't see us, either. One-way glass," Larsen explained.

"What's the purpose of all this?"

"Well, Drisbane," the general began, "I was up all night trying to think of new methods of testing Ms. Flanagan to understand her abilities. At some point, it occurred to me that she may have been compromised by Carver in some way, with or without her knowledge. Perhaps that would explain her unique abilities; perhaps it's something he did to her," Larsen paused, taking a long sip from the cup of coffee he carried with him. "I don't know, though, and I don't know if *she* knows. All of our tests for physical evidence of any anomalies are coming up blank, and I don't know her well enough to be able to tell if there are any mental anomalies at play. So I thought, we have to see what makes her tick. What's going on in her head. Only then can we know if Carver did anything to her, mentally."

"I....." Steven was at a loss for words. "How?"

"Simple interrogation, boy. The old good cop, bad cop routine. You've already got a good start on your role, the way you reassured her just now."

Steven felt an inexplicable flicker of guilt as he realized his attempt to make Deanna feel better was playing into whatever new game this was. "What exactly is my role, sir?"

"Today, you just observe. There are cameras in there, so you don't have to sit here; you can watch on your Wand, if you like. You won't have any direct involvement with the interrogation until tomorrow. I will let you know when I need you."

With a growing feeling of unease, Steven nodded, and watched as the General entered the tiny, cell-like room where Deanna sat. Although he had deep misgivings about this new tactic, he knew better than to question orders.

<u>Benjamin</u>

General Benjamin Larsen had spent the entire night staring at the ceiling, in his quarters. He felt terribly, inexplicably lost. It was a feeling that had been growing inside him for years, ever since Carver had left. He felt utterly disconnected, as if he wasn't really sure who he was or what his reason for being was. He had channeled it, as well as he could, into keeping the organization going and trying to find his old friend.

Larsen had given his entire life to the organization. He never married or had children, or even much of a social life at all. Carver had been his only real friend, and Benjamin was fine with that. He believed so strongly in their work and their mission, he didn't feel he needed friends.

Of course, his loneliness had been magnified during the years in which he unsuccessfully searched for Carver. He pushed it to the side, though, and rationalized that he was simply upset about his former friend's status as a possible threat to the organization (and the world at large).

For some reason, though, this woman, this Deanna, exacerbated the feeling of being lost. He could barely think straight; it was almost as if his thoughts were not his own. He found that as his feelings of displacement and disconnection worsened, so too did an inexplicable feeling of hostility he was developing toward the woman. He found that the more time he spent with her, and the more research he did on her, the more he felt she was simply not worthy of having met Carver. She had somehow, through some trick of life, been able to achieve by accident what he had strived for for so many years – she had found David Carver. Benjamin resented her deeply for that.

Carver had not only been his only friend, he had been his mentor. Benjamin had almost worshipped the man, spending every waking second trying to soak up his genius. He had lived in constant amazement at his superior's ideas and methods. He strove daily to be more like Carver. When he learned Carver meditated, he took up the practice. When he learned Carver had stopped meditating, he also stopped. If he learned Carver enjoyed a food, he would incorporate it into his diet; if Carver didn't like something, Benjamin would reject it, as well. He modeled every aspect of his life after Carver's example.

When Carver began to inexplicably deteriorate, Benjamin felt like his world was falling apart. He researched the other man's symptoms and tried to formulate magical cures, but nothing worked. He recruited doctors and healers from around the world to examine his friend, but no one seemed to be able to find a cure. He knew that if he had even a tenth of the knowledge and ability that Carver had had, he could solve the problem; however, he also knew that he, Benjamin Larsen, was no David Carver.

He had not yet been able to forgive himself for that failure. However, he tried to channel his anger toward himself into finding Carver. He thought that if only he could find him, he would have another chance at saving him. He could make up for his earlier failure.

For nearly eighteen years, now, he had been searching for Carver. At some point, his intentions started becoming cloudy. He found that he was afraid to hope he would find his friend, because his hope kept getting shattered. The constant heartbreak and self-doubt he experienced were getting to be too much. He started to fear that Carver was no longer the man he had known, and that he could even be a threat. In some ways, it was easier to accept that his former mentor was now a threat than it was to accept that he, Benjamin, had failed his friend.

Of course, there were other responsibilities to keep him occupied, to distract him from his feelings of guilt and heartache. For one thing, he had to keep the organization going, so that Carver's work would not have been in vain. Then, in his minimal free time, he had to keep Carver's motorcycle running and road-ready, so it would be ready for him when he got back. He just had to keep busy, be productive, and work for the greater good. Then he would be forgiven for failing his friend.

He felt like he had been on the right track, starting this little team with Drisbane and Eric and John. Everything about it just seemed to fall into place so effortlessly, from finding Drisbane to recruiting the techs. Though progress wasn't going as quickly as he'd like, he felt like they were getting close, somehow. At least he had someone to share his mission with, now. It helped to have other people working with him for a common goal.

And then, this woman showed up.

Why did she see through the shields? An anomaly, for sure. But then, more importantly – why had she been allowed, through mere circumstance, to achieve the goal that had been eluding him for so long? Why had she been allowed to meet and talk with David Carver?

It was mind-boggling.

As the night dragged on, Larsen formulated wild theories that whatever external forces had corrupted the mind of his hero may also be at work in Miss Flanagan's life. Then, he remembered the many test results which showed her to be utterly ordinary, and he told himself he was being silly. He couldn't shake the feeling, though, that she was somehow deceiving them, impossible though that may be.

He wondered if Carver himself could have worked some magic on the woman, caused some invisible anomaly in her mind to prevent her from sharing information about him. That seemed a slightly more valid notion. He realized he didn't know enough about her, and spent the rest of the night studying every detail of her life that he could dig up by either magical or governmental means.

Every detail he learned about her life caused him to feel even more resentment and jealousy toward her, but he did not let his emotions deter him. He came up with what he saw as the most logical plan of action: they would simply interrogate her, and get to the bottom of what she had that he didn't have... in the most rational sense, of course.

Deanna

It seemed to be an unreasonably long time that she sat alone, in that tiny room, staring at the dark, shiny panes in front of her. She knew, because she had just seen the room from the outside, that Steven and General Larsen could see her; however, she could see nothing but her own reflection. The light hanging over her head was intensely bright, causing her to squint a bit. She felt quite powerless, more than a little afraid, and utterly hopeless.

The door opened and General Larsen entered, wearing a grim expression on his previously jovial face. He didn't speak to her or even look at her, instead glancing around the tiny room and murmuring to himself, "This won't do," before producing a Wand from his pocket and tapping on the screen. A large, comfortable armchair appeared in the corner. The general sat in it with a contented sigh, arranged his clipboard and coffee around him, and finally turned his attention to Deanna on her tiny, uncomfortable plastic chair.

"So, Miss Flanagan," he said, in a tone that reminded Deanna strongly of the character Agent Smith in that movie "The Matrix" that Barb the librarian was always watching, "It is 'Miss,' isn't it? No spouse?"

"Correct."

"Why is that? Most women your age are married."

"Just never found the right guy, I guess."

"Really?" Larsen glanced at the papers on his clipboard. "You're thirty-seven years old, and you 'haven't found the right guy'? Doesn't that seem like a bit of a cop out?"

Deanna was beginning to feel irritated by this line of questioning. She clung to that feeling, because it felt better than being lost and afraid. "What exactly are you trying to say, General?"

"Just seems to me there may be a deeper reason for your solitary state. How long has it been since you've been in a relationship?"

"A few years," she answered, defensively.

"It's been a few YEARS? Doesn't that get lonely? Haven't you dated at all?"

"There was…. Someone… last year. We didn't really date," she admitted. "It's kind of a long story."

"Well, Ms. Flanagan, we have all day."

"What exactly is the point of talking about my romantic history?"

"We need to understand who you are as a whole, in order to understand why you have these strange gifts. This seems as good a place to start as any. So tell me, who was this 'someone' you didn't date last year?"

She heaved a deep sigh. "His name is Louis."

"And where did you meet Louis?" Larsen asked, drawing out the two syllables.

"He was the head bartender at the restaurant I worked in at that time."

"Ah, an affair with your boss. Always a good plan," the general said, his voice dripping with sarcasm.

"It wasn't an affair. It was an ill-advised one night stand," Deanna's voice was hollow. Her anger was being drowned by a sea of hopelessness as she realized her only way out of this place was to comply with the General and answer his questions. "I had liked him for a really long time. He texted me one night to come over. Things happened. When he thought I was asleep, he kept chugging from a glass he hid under the bed when I rolled over. Turned out to be straight vodka. He was relapsing after four years sober."

"I see. You think his decision to have relations with you stemmed from the same thought processes that caused him to relapse? Perhaps some need to punish himself resulted in inviting you over that night."

Deanna shrugged, feeling very small. It was deeply uncomfortable discussing all of this with a stranger; it wasn't something she had discussed with anyone else. The fact that Larsen's line of questioning closely aligned with the sense of self-loathing she had so often tried to tune out did not help matters.

"Have you ever had a more serious relationship? Long-term? Or has it been all one-night stands and flings?"

"Of COURSE I've had long-term relationships, and I don't appreciate the implication that I am in any way promiscuous." She embraced the tiny spark of anger that made her feel as if she still had any power over the situation.

"Didn't realize I was implying that, but you do seem a bit sensitive about the issue. How many men HAVE you been with, Miss Flanagan?"

"That's really none of your business."

He checked his papers again. "We know of fifteen."

"I... what? What do you mean, you know of fifteen? How do you even research that?"

"You should realize by now that we have more methodology at our disposal than any other organization on Earth, Miss Flanagan. We know everything about you. My goal is to find out what you know about yourself."

She stared at him, open-mouthed. She had no words to express how utterly violated she felt.

"So tell me, Miss Flanagan. Why do you think your relationship with – "he paused as he checked his papers once again, "with Mike ended in 2008?"

"You... you know about everyone I've ever dated?"

"Oh yes, quite. We know everything about you," Larsen said casually. "Like that little trip to the mental hospital when you were sixteen. Failed attempt at suicide, eh? What did that feel like?"

The color drained out of Deanna's face, and her voice sounded like a hollow monotone in her own ears. "Obviously not good."

"But what did it really *feel* like? I mean, you had reached the conclusion that the world would be better off without you, and made the decision to end your own life. AND YOU FAILED!" Larsen bellowed the last part; Deanna felt like the words were physical blows. She flinched slightly. "I'd imagine you had to deal with a lot of dark feelings, in that mental hospital," Larsen continued, more quietly. "What was it like?"

"It wasn't the best time of my life," Deanna's voice came out as a near whisper. She felt like every dark thought and fear she'd ever had had manifested as this man in front of her, and there was nothing she could do to tune him out if she ever wanted to return home.

"Miss Flanagan, you must be able to articulate a little better than that. I'm asking what really went on in your head while you were in the mental hospital."

She stared at her own reflection in the glass in front of her, not really seeing. "I felt like my entire life was a waste," she murmured. "I felt like I was nothing but a drain on my parents, my loved ones, and the world in general. I felt like a disease that needed to be eradicated from the planet, but there was no cure, no relief. I was just infecting the world."

"Ahhh," Larsen said, making some notes on his clipboard. "That's a bit more eloquent. Tell me, how did you overcome these feelings? Or did you ever?"

"I.....I, um...." Deanna stammered. "I did a lot of mental work, over the years. Meditation. Affirmations. Things like that."

"And you think it worked?"

"For the most part. I still have to work on not getting too down on myself." Deanna wished she could have a few minutes alone to work

71

on some breathing exercises and affirmations, right then. She desperately needed that reassurance, that feeling of connecting with something larger and knowing everything would be ok.

Larsen nodded. For several long minutes, he stared at her, silently. She was beginning to feel like an insect under his scrutiny when he said, in a distracted tone that seemed not entirely directed at her, "I wonder if this ongoing process of self-delusion has somehow caused the ability to see through magical shields."

"I don't.... I don't understand what you mean."

"Quite. I'm just wondering if these 'affirmations' and whatnot have somehow deluded you into believing in a false reality. Perhaps you have hypnotized yourself to a point of not being able to see what really exists, such as our shields."

"Are you... are you saying the thoughts I had in the hospital were reality?" Deanna's voice was hushed, and bordered on the brink between anger and tears.

"Not sure yet, I have to check some test results from yesterday," Larsen said. "You sit tight, I'll be back when I'm done."

He left the little room, leaving Deanna alone. She barely noticed the tear that ran down her own cheek as she stared into nothingness, desperately trying to get control over her thoughts.

David

He was suddenly very aware of the fact that he was freezing.

As he stood hugging himself, wondering why he was so cold, David looked around the street on which he stood. Something had changed.

He peered around, taking stock of what was around him, then he realized all the people were gone. There had been all sorts of people bustling around, before; now it was just him, alone, on the sidewalk. The gargoyle who had given him that hot cup of liquid comfort was gone. Everyone was gone. Where had they all gone?

He wished he could go someplace else, too. This place had gotten so damn cold.

As he watched, the world around him lost color. The blue sky turned a pale, cloudy grey. The building facades — red brick, various colors of vinyl siding, white cinder block — all faded to shades of grey. Soon, everything around him was grey, and he stood shivering on the silent sidewalk, looking around wildly for some light, some comfort. This place had felt so safe, before; now it just hurt.

For some time, he felt only the cold, the loneliness, and the pain. Then, gradually, he became aware of a glow in the distance. It was as if there were a warm, golden light emanating from somewhere behind the now-grey buildings. He could not quite see what it was or from whence it came, but it looked warm. He shuffled off down the street, toward the golden glow. It seemed to move further away as he walked toward it, but he followed it anyway, determined to find its source.

Steven

Steven watched the interrogation on his Wand, in his quarters. He was rather surprised; he had never seen this side of the General before. Larsen's cold and at times cruel behavior toward Deanna made Steven feel unsettled and deeply uncomfortable. He knew, though, that his unsettled feelings must stem from a lack of understanding of his superior officer's methods. He knew the General would never act irrationally or with bad intentions.

When he saw Larsen head toward the door, he Broomed to meet him outside the little cell. He glanced at Deanna through the glass and felt a pang of guilt at her apparent abject misery, but did his best not to let his feelings show as he greeted the General.

"Sir," he said with a nod.

"Drisbane, you didn't have to come. Like I said, I won't need you today, just want you to observe."

Steven shrugged, not knowing what to say.

"It's going well, I think," Larsen continued.

"Is it, sir?"

"Haven't you been observing?"

"Yes, sir. I have. It's odd, seeing you behave like that," Steven admitted.

"It's a role, Ensign, just a role. For her good just as much as ours."

"How so?"

"Well," Larsen began, then sighed thoughtfully. "Do you remember boot camp?"

"Yessir. Not my favorite memories."

"Ha!" The general clapped Steven on the shoulder as he barked a laugh. "For none of us, my boy. But it was necessary to be broken down in that way before we could be built back up as better men."

Steven considered this for a moment. He wasn't completely sure that he was a better man than he had been before enlisting. He was older, certainly, and wiser, but he attributed that more to the organization and the passage of time than he did to boot camp. For the most part, he considered boot camp an unpleasant hurdle one had to overcome in order to prove one's commitment to enlisting. He certainly wasn't sure it had helped him in any way. It had just been a necessary evil to get to where he now was.

"I'm not really sure I follow you, sir," he said aloud.

74

Larsen gave him a long, considering look that went on for a second longer than Steven was comfortable with. His hand started twitching as he waited for the General to say something. Finally, the older man said, "Miss Flanagan suffers from some pretty serious self-esteem issues, I'm sure you've noticed. She has dealt with them in her own way, but it may be more effective to break her down to the nuts and bolts, and let her see she's still there, still standing."

Nodding slowly, Steven said, "Like some kind of immersion therapy, almost." He wanted to believe this, but felt a bit as if he were trying to convince himself.

"Precisely. Also, I'm wondering if Carver could have done something to her brain, to compromise her. To prevent her from sharing any pertinent information about him. The only way to find that out is to really get inside her head and see what makes her tick."

Steven digested all of this. When he looked at it in this light, he was able to see that Larsen's seemingly abusive behavior toward Deanna was really for the greater good, as he had known it would be. It would benefit not only the organization, but Deanna herself. It was a necessary evil, just like boot camp had been. He nodded once, firmly, and said, "I understand now, sir."

"Good man," the general said, jovially. "Now I must confer with the techs, then get back to it. You continue observing, and enjoy some well-deserved down time."

"Thank you, sir," Steven answered, feeling suddenly tired. "I will."

Back in his quarters, Steven lay on his bed and stared at the screen of his Wand, where he saw Deanna's now tear-stained face as she waited for General Larsen to return. He found he was having a hard time keeping his eyes open, but he struggled to do so. Eventually, he must have lost the battle, because the next thing he knew, he was dreaming.

In his dream, he stood in a long hall. There were people standing throughout the hall, some of whom he recognized; General Larsen was there, and Carver ... even John and Eric, the techs. No one moved, though; they simply stood around in this giant hall, as still and silent as statues. With perfect dream logic, Steven figured he should do the same, though he wasn't sure why.

After a moment, he noticed a light coming from somewhere behind him, growing brighter by the second. Unable to resist his curiosity, he turned toward the light, and saw it was coming from Deanna. She was standing on some sort of a platform in the center of the hall, a bit higher up than everyone else, and she was *glowing*. Though she, too, stood perfectly still, a light seemed to radiate from within her. Within seconds, she was glowing as brightly as the sun, and he had to shield his eyes. As he did so, he experienced a sense of vertigo and peeked between his fingers. He realized he was moving, being pulled toward Deanna as if by some magnetic force. A quick glance around him showed him that everyone was being pulled toward her.

Unable to resist, he allowed himself to be pulled by this unseen current, and then found he was enveloped into that bright, golden light. It was like flying into the sun. The shock of being completely engulfed into that bright glow caused him to breathe in sharply, which woke him up.

He sat up and glanced at the clock. Only five minutes had passed; he hadn't missed anything important. A quick glance at his Wand showed him that Larsen was only now returning to the cell to resume interrogating Deanna. That was a relief.

Steven sat up and shook his head, trying to shake the strange feeling the dream had left in him. He focused on watching the interview on his wand and tried to put the dream out of his mind.

Eric

Eric was at his computer, as he almost always was, scanning days' worth of data from the Eyes. There was currently no visible trace of Carver, in Woodford or anywhere else on Earth.

"I'm bored," John announced from across the room. Eric ignored him.

After a few minutes passed, John continued, "I don't know why you keep looking at that garbage, anyway. There's no sign of him."

"It's weird," Eric mumbled back. "I just feel like we're missing something."

General Larsen suddenly materialized next to John, causing both techs to jump slightly. John nearly fell off his chair. Recovering himself, he frowned at the General and said, "There are doors, y'know. You don't strictly HAVE to use the Broom to enter a room."

"Gentlemen," Larsen said in greeting, ignoring John's comment. "How goes it?"

"Nothing new," Eric answered, barely glancing away from the screen.

"That's okay," the General assured him. "I actually want you to turn your attention to Miss Flanagan, at the moment. Run some scans on her today, and compare them to the test results from yesterday. I'm particularly interested in her brain activity and energy signatures. Just curious if there are any changes. Actually, keep an eye on her molecular structure, too. Keep an eye on everything about her. Let me know if there are any changes from yesterday, or if you find any anomalies at all."

Eric shrugged and nodded, while John sighed and rolled his eyes.

"Good men," Larsen stated, then pushed the button on his Broom and vanished.

"That's all you, bro," John said, drily.

Eric was already tapping away at his keyboard, running scans of Deanna in her cell. He began analyzing the data, paying particular attention to the specific intangibles the General had mentioned. He compared the new scans with those of the day before. After a few moments, he pulled up a visual scan of the subject's molecular energy output, and another from the day before. He stared at the nearly-identical images for a few moments before murmuring, "Hey, do you see that?"

John did not turn away from the video game he was currently playing. "Nope."

Eric stared at the screen for a few moments, then rubbed his eyes and shook his head, deciding he was overtired.

For a second, he had thought he saw Carver's energy signature flickering around Deanna's molecular energy. He knew that was impossible, though; energy signatures were created by the presence of a living being, and how could Carver have been inside the actual molecules that the woman was comprised of?

Still, it was odd. He thought he'd better inform the General, even if it was just fatigue causing him to imagine things. He should get a second opinion from someone in charge.

He checked Larsen's location and watched him interview Deanna for a moment, waiting for an opportune time to interrupt. After watching for a few minutes, he decided he'd better not bother the General with such an improbable and weird observation until he was in a better mood.

Across the desk from him, John leaned over with a curious expression, having overheard Larsen's interview with Deanna coming from Eric's Wand. Quietly, he tuned his own device to the interview, too, and the two techs watched in silence.

Deanna

Deanna was beginning to feel nauseous.

She had felt alternately terrified, irritated, frustrated, aghast, horrified, and emotionally crippled since today's interrogation had begun. However, since her current experience and its duration depended on General Larsen's mercy, at this point, she had no outlet for any of the above feelings. So, they all settled in her stomach as a churning sea of nausea while she tried to navigate his seemingly never-ending stream of terrible, prying questions and comments about some of her darkest and most personal experiences.

"Tell me about your parents, Miss Flanagan," the General's voice sounded much further away than it should. He was sitting not two feet away from her, but the sea of thoughts, emotions, and now physical illness inside her separated her focus from him, making him seem further away.

"Don't you already know?" she responded numbly. "I'm sure you've checked them out, too."

"Yes," the General said bluntly, "but I'd like to know your feelings about them."

"I love them. Obviously. They're my parents."

"So you love them because of shared DNA?"

She closed her eyes for a second, willing the annoyance she felt not to come out in her voice. "It's more than that, I'm sure you know. They are my parents. They created me, they helped me become the person I am."

"Yes, for better or worse, I suppose that's true." Larsen looked at his notes again. "I see they also loaned you a considerable amount of money just a few months ago?"

She already knew they knew everything about her, and felt like the shock of that fact should have worn off by now. However, Larsen's words made her heart feel like it had been replaced by a balled up fist. Her throat suddenly tightened around the lump that was forming inside of it, rendering her unable to speak, so she simply nodded. She hated the fact that he knew about what felt like one of her biggest failures in recent history.

"I imagine this was because of your unemployed state? You are unable to support yourself?"

She nodded again, swallowing hard and fighting the tears that threatened to spill out from behind her eyes.

"Have you considered applying for some kind of assistance? There is government aid, in this country, for people like you."

Blinking away her tears, Deanna croaked, "I don't need that kind of help. I just need to find a job."

"But, Miss Flanagan, perhaps it is time to consider that you are simply not equipped to be a functioning member of society. Most people don't have enforced trips to mental hospitals in their adolescent years. Surely, if you were able, you would have found a suitable career by your advanced age. You are moving rapidly toward forty, you know. Do you really think waiting tables and pouring cocktails is adequate employment for an adult?"

She realized there was no use fighting her own body as her tears burned her eyes. "I'm able to work, I'm fine. And I'm going to get out of the restaurant industry, I think. I'm thinking lately I may be burned out. I think there's something else for me out there. I just haven't found my path yet." These phrases that she had told herself time and time again tumbled out of her mouth, almost unbidden. "Some people are just late bloomers." Her voice sounded hollow and empty to her own ears as she recited the words that usually comforted her.

"Oh, dear. Do you really believe that?" Larsen sounded vaguely amused.

"Julia Child didn't even start cooking 'til she was forty," Deanna continued. It was an encouraging tidbit of information that her father had recently told her, and to which she clung in her darkest moments of self-doubt. "General Sanders didn't start selling chicken until he was over forty. There's no deadline to success."

Larsen's response was a long, hearty laugh. He actually laughed so hard that he had to take off his glasses and wipe his eyes before saying, "You really have done a number on yourself, with these self-delusions." He paused for a moment to catch his breath and shake his head slowly. "This is as good a time as any to take a break, I suppose. I need to come up with a strategy to try and help you fix all of the mental damage you've done to yourself."

"It's not mental damage," she protested weakly.

He heaved a sigh as he stood up. "The fact that you don't see it that way only proves that it is, Miss Flanagan." He removed his Wand from his pocket and tapped away at the screen. His comfortable armchair disappeared, and a toilet and sink appeared in their place. There were no walls or door around them, and they were immediately in front of the one way glass wall that provided no privacy. "Clean yourself up and do whatever you need to do. We will resume our talk in a bit."

The general left the little room. Deanna stared at the toilet and sink for a moment, then at her reflection in the glass. After a few minutes, she broke into sobs.

Benjamin

General Larsen wasn't feeling himself, at all. He felt so "not himself" that he almost felt dizzy.

He had taken on this "bad cop" role with every intention of doing good. He simply wanted to understand this woman, her gifts, and her connection to Carver. Granted, he had some irrational hostility toward the woman, but he was man enough to put aside such emotions and work for the greater good. He wanted to understand why she had, by random occurrence, gotten to meet Carver even though the organization, with all of the tools at their disposal, hadn't been able to find him for nearly eighteen years.

That was all. No more, no less. He wanted to work for the greater good. It was his calling, as he often told himself, to work for the greater good, to keep the organization going in Carver's absence. He just wanted to figure out what made this woman unique, and use whatever it was to help him find Carver.

As he immersed himself in the "bad cop" role, though, he found it was coming to him rather naturally. If he stopped to think about it, he would find it unsettling; however, he had no time for self-reflection. He had to return to the task at hand. The mission always came first.

He was running on pure instinct, at this point, and his instincts were telling him Deanna's lifetime of bad decisions and self-delusions had left her too confused to allow him to understand why she had been allowed to meet David Carver. If he was going to be able to understand the real her, the nuts and bolts, he'd have to wipe all of that nonsense away.

"Tabula rasa," he thought to himself, and he began to formulate a plan.

As he walked down the hall, he found he had a little extra skip in his step.

Deanna

The door opened and Larsen re-entered the room. Deanna sat on the floor, now, hugging her knees; it was easier than trying to find a comfortable position in that horrible little chair. She stared up at the General, silently, with fear and loathing in her eyes.

"Good news, Miss Flanagan," he said as he stepped over her and tapped at his Wand. The toilet and sink disappeared, and the comfortable chair reappeared. He sank into it with a grunt, then turned toward her. "I've figured out how to fix you up."

Deanna sniffed and wiped her face. She was feeling so low that his words had no emotional impact on her one way or the other. She shrugged a shoulder half-heartedly.

"Do you hear me, girl? I know how to fix you! Get excited!"

She continued staring at him blankly.

He heaved a sigh and said, "Pull yourself together. Come on, sit in the chair. You're not an animal. Sit with me and have a conversation like a human being."

She pulled herself into a standing position and flopped into the chair, obediently. After a second, she pulled her legs up onto the chair and resumed hugging her knees.

"Miss Flanagan, I believe that whatever the reasons for your unique abilities are, we can't find them because of all of the mental and emotional garbage you have hanging around in there," Larsen explained, tapping his temple to illustrate what he meant by "in there."

"'K," Deanna was unable to muster more than a monosyllabic response.

"We can fix that, though. With the technology at our disposal, we can use the energy to wipe all of that unnecessary garbage away. It would be a fresh start for you, unburdened by feelings of guilt, remorse, and self-loathing. You would have a clean slate from which to rebuild yourself."

She blinked slowly, trying to process what he had just said. Her brow furrowed. "You want... you're going to... wait. You're going to brain wash me?"

"Ha!" Larsen barked. "I suppose, in a sense, we will be washing your brain. But that has such negative connotations, and this is such a positive thing. A fresh start, Miss Flanagan! Free from your many past mistakes and self-delusions!"

Deanna sat up a little straighter and lowered her feet to the floor. Cold, icy fear coursed through her, awakening her sense of alertness. "I don't want that," she said with unwavering certainty. "I don't want that at all. You can't do that."

The General sighed. "Come now, Miss Flanagan. Think about it. One thing I've run into again and again while interviewing you is your overwhelming sense of unworthiness. You clearly have some serious self-esteem problems, and guilt over past mistakes, no matter how much you cover them with affirmations and platitudes. We can fix that. We can take away all the parts of yourself that you dislike."

"I... I like myself just fine as I am," she stammered. As she said it, she realized she meant it wholeheartedly. All of her familiar self-doubt and loathing disappeared in the face of this new threat. She did not want to be changed. She wanted to be exactly who she was.

He chuckled in response. "That is a fear response, driven by your fear of change. It's natural, I suppose, but I'm sure if you give the matter some thought, you will see that I'm right."

She mutely shook her head as terror pierced her heart like an icicle.

Shaking his head with the kind of disbelieving wonder one displays when watching a rambunctious child, Larsen stood. He stated, with great confidence, "You just need some rest. Sleep on it, you'll feel better about things." He tapped the screen of his Wand, and the chair underneath her was suddenly an equally uncomfortable cot. His own, comfortable chair vanished, and were replaced by the toilet and sink. "I will be back in the morning, and we will give you your wonderful, fresh start."

He pushed the button on his Broom and blinked out of existence, leaving Deanna in a state of burgeoning panic.

She sat, staring at her reflection in the glass, for a very long time. Her mind raced.

Larsen was not entirely wrong, of course. She had always had self-esteem issues. She acknowledged that. However, she had always felt like it was something she could overcome, that she WOULD overcome. She was simply finding her path in the world. Sometimes it was hard, but it was supposed to be, right? That's how life shapes your character. Overcoming one's flaws and weaknesses was how one grew as a person, she'd always thought.

Maybe she couldn't always see how life was shaping her character for the better, and of course she often had doubts, but...

Erasing her personality seemed a bit extreme.

If that was even what he meant, that is. He had been a little vague, really, with all of his talk about a clean slate and erasing her regrets and so on. What, exactly, were they going to do to her?

Would she even be herself anymore?

Would she even be more than a vegetable?

It was amazing, really, she thought. All her life, her mind had wandered down these paths of self-loathing, unbidden and despite her best efforts. She could rattle off a list of her flaws without a moment's thought, but found it difficult to think of even one thing she liked about herself.

Until now.

Suddenly, as she pondered the impending loss of herself, her positive attributes seemed innumerable.

"Will he take away my creativity? My empathy? My memories with family and friends? My imagination? My motivation? My optimism? What will be left of me?"

She closed her eyes and willed herself to be calm. Now, more than ever, she needed to feel the calm of being connected to something greater than herself. She began the process of releasing her thoughts and entering a meditative state.

Benjamin

He was completely unsurprised to find Steven waiting in his quarters.

"Sir," the boy blurted, standing as Benjamin entered the room, "I'm sorry to bother you, and I know it must be for the greater good, but can you please help me understand how erasing her mind will help our mission?"

"Of course, Drisbane, of course. As always, you only need to ask," Benjamin answered jovially, his eyes twinkling. "Why continue trying to break through her many self-delusions and defenses to see what brought Carver to her, and what he may have done to her? The energy gives us the ability to dispense with all of this nonsense and get right to the heart of the matter. And God knows it will help her, too. Poor woman's just a mental mess."

"But... but...wouldn't we be playing God a bit too much, sir? What if we're messing with the natural order of things? What if she becomes some kind of vegetable or zombie or...or..."

"Calm down, Drisbane. It's not as if I'm going to completely delete her. We're just going to... edit her, a bit."

"Edit?" Steven's voice came out as a high-pitched squeak.

"We do it all the time, boy. How many times have we altered reality, ever so slightly, to improve circumstances for our countrymen?"

Steven's mouth opened and closed several times as he remembered his studies on organization activity throughout the years.

"We are helping this woman, Drisbane," Benjamin continued. "I know you're developing some kind of an attachment to her, I can tell. I understand. You found her and brought her in, after all. You must feel partially responsible for all this. You should thus be that much more enthusiastic about this opportunity to free her from her personal demons. We're giving her a second chance at life. Many people would relish the opportunity."

"I don't... I'm not...." Steven stammered. "I just want to make sure we're doing the right thing, sir."

"Have we ever not? It's as you told the woman when we first encountered her: we're the good guys," Benjamin answered him gently, remembering how young and inexperienced the Ensign was. "Sometimes the right thing is the hardest thing to do, my boy. Your questions and commitment to the greater good are admirable, and I applaud you for them. I'm sure that you will feel better about everything once you've given it some thought. Now, I need to get some rest."

The younger man nodded and stepped toward the door.

"Oh, and Drisbane," Benjamin called after him. "I'd like you to bring her breakfast in the morning. Put her mind at ease a bit. Be the good cop, so to speak. It won't be good for any of us if she's all panicky and skittish when we do the procedure."

"Yes, sir," Steven answered, then left the General's quarters.

Benjamin slept, and dreamed.

In his dream, he was lost in utter darkness. He could see nothing, but stumbled forward with the aid of a staff he held in his hands, which he used to tap the ground ahead of him as he made his way. The ground was hard, and he sensed that he was indoors, but that was all he could glean from his slow progress through complete and utter darkness.

Eventually, his staff made contact with something hard. Stone. It was tall, nearly his own height. He felt it with his hands, and came to the conclusion that it was a statue. He could not tell what, exactly, it was a statue of.

He continued his slow progress, occasionally bumping into other statues. His eyes did not adjust to the complete and utter darkness.

Suddenly, quite unexpectedly, a bright light appeared immediately in front of him. The sphere of illumination showed him the statues around him, all broken and missing pieces. The light itself appeared over the statue of a woman, missing its head.

As he took everything in, the light grew brighter and brighter. It hurt his eyes. He swung his staff at it, blindly, wanting only to stop the pain in his eyes. Though he missed the light, he made contact with the statue, and it immediately crumbled to dust. The light began to fade.

He glanced around and saw all of the other statues were crumbling to dust, as well. He vaguely wondered if that was supposed to happen.

His staff crashed to the floor, and he looked down at his own hand. It, too, was turning to dust. He looked down at himself and watched, in horror, as his body crumbled and fell away.

As the last pieces fell, he awoke, safe in his own bed. He lay awake for a few moments, unsettled by the nightmare, before rolling over and falling into a fitful but dreamless sleep.

Steven

At first light, Steven entered Deanna's cell with a tray of food in his hand. He found her sitting up straight on the edge of her cot, with her feet on the ground and her eyes closed. She showed no reaction to the sound of the door closing, so he cleared his throat loudly.

She opened her eyes.

"Good morning," he said, awkwardly. "Were you sleeping? That can't be a comfortable way to sleep."

"No," she answered. He wasn't sure if she meant she hadn't been sleeping, or hadn't been comfortable.

"Well, I brought you some breakfast," he stated cheerfully, proffering the tray. She made no move to take it, so he placed it next to her on the cot, and sat down on the other side of her. He tried desperately to think of a conversation opener, and finally settled on, "How are you feeling this morning, Deanna?"

She glanced at him with a withering expression that made him feel like he was shrinking. He rallied and tried again. "Did you sleep well?"

"Didn't sleep at all," she whispered.

"Ah, I see," he said, then stared at his feet for several long seconds while he tried to think of something to say. "I guess you're a little nervous about the procedure?"

A tear trickled down her face, then another. She did not look at him.

"Don't cry," he murmured, putting a hand on her back in what he hoped was a comforting gesture. "It will be a good thing, I promise."

Finally, she turned toward him. "Remember when I first got here?" she asked, her tone bitter. "You said I would not be harmed while I was here. Your promises are pretty meaningless, it would seem." Tears continued to flow down her face.

Steven didn't know what to say. He felt terribly uncomfortable in the face of her tears, and didn't know how to make her see that the procedure would be good not only for her, but for everyone. If only the General were here to tell him what to say. He was alone, though, and he just wanted to make her stop crying. He found himself pulling her into his arms. He hugged her tight, and patted her back, hoping it would make her feel better.

After a few moments, she put a hand on his chest, fumbled for a moment, and then pushed him away. Her face was damp, but no new tears fell.

"Thanks," she whispered.

"No need for thanks. I'm always here to give a hug to a lady in need," he said lightly.

Her voice sounded hollow and expressionless as she said, "Oh, I wasn't thanking you for the hug. I was thanking you for this."

She held up the Broom that he suddenly realized was no longer in his chest pocket.

"Deanna —"he began, but she pushed the button and vanished, leaving him alone in her cell.

He stared at thin air for a moment, willing her to reappear, to no avail. A sinking feeling developed in his stomach as he realized she was actually gone. He was pretty certain the General would not be happy with him.

David

David had been traveling toward the glow in the sky for what seemed like a very, very long time. He had walked and walked until he came to a pile of icy, black rocks, which he had started to climb. He had been climbing for hours, now; the pile was much larger than it appeared. As he climbed, he realized it could really be called a mountain.

The glow now appeared to be coming from just over the peak. He tried to ignore the frigid cold as he rose slowly, handhold by handhold, foothold by foothold. It was slippery with ice, and terribly slow going, but he persevered.

Finally, after hours of slow, suffering progress, he reached up a hand to find his next handhold and found what felt like warm sand. He looked around at the icy rocks to which he clung and thought vaguely that warm sand wouldn't fit in this scenario.

He reached up as far as he could, bringing both hands to the top of the rock and immersing them in the warm sand, then he pulled the rest of his body up. It took every ounce of strength in his freezing, exhausted body, but he succeeded and found himself laying on a stretch of warm, golden sand. For a while, he just lay there, enjoying the warmth and catching his breath.

When he felt able to do so, he rolled onto his side and noticed there was a long stretch of smooth, black road at the end of the sand. On the other side of the road was more sand, being kissed by the incoming tide of beautiful, azure ocean waves. He admired the view for a few moments, before pulling himself into a standing position.

As he stood, he noticed a gorgeous, gleaming, brand new motorcycle standing where the sand met the road. He grinned as he ran toward it, knowing his keys would be in the ignition.

Deanna

Deanna had no idea how the Broom actually worked, but she had seen Steven and Larsen use theirs multiple times. It appeared to be as simple as pushing a button. She closed her eyes, pictured home, and pushed the button, praying all the while that it was as simple as it had looked.

A wave of vertigo, then all-consuming cold. She stumbled on snowy, slippery ground as she opened her eyes, which put her directly in the path of four young men who were walking toward her. She stared at them, wide eyed and terrified, wondering where she was.

"Get out the way," she heard one of the young men mutter. She looked around, wildly. Everything was covered with snow, piles of it, as if there had been a blizzard which was shoveled and plowed off to the sides, then more snow started falling. The piles of snow left a very narrow walkway, which was, itself, slippery with freshly falling snow.

"Hey, it's your world, lady, we're just living in it," another young man said, with a snarky tone, and then the four of them pushed past her. She heard them laughing as they walked away, leaving her sitting in a pile of snow.

As she took stock of her surroundings, she realized she was actually standing between two buildings. She glanced upwards and saw familiar trellises, now white and sparkly with snow and icicles, and a sob of relief escaped her. She was in Woodford. She was in the walkway that led to the laundromat, the same place where she had met the robed man mere days earlier. It seemed like a lifetime ago, now.

She hadn't planned on stealing Steven's Broom. She had not been able to sleep at all, so she spent the whole night meditating. She had simply kept her mind clear. When thoughts arose, she focused on feeling free and safe, and on the awareness that she could overcome any situation. She extended her awareness out into the universe and repeated affirmations all night long.

As the result of all of that, she had felt much calmer by the time Steven entered the room. However, his presence reminded her of the reality of the situation which she faced, and she was terribly overtired; perhaps that's why she had wept.

When he hugged her, she felt deeply uncomfortable. She did not want him to hold her; she did not want to share a moment of intimacy with someone she had come to think of as one of the bad guys. However, as she moved to push him away, she felt the Broom in his pocket, and suddenly everything made sense.

It had been a purely impulsive move, but it seemed to have worked. She was back in her hometown. She was freezing and sorely underdressed for the weather, but she was HOME.

"But I've got to keep moving," she thought. "They'll be after me in seconds."

She decided to stop at her apartment and dress a bit more appropriately for the weather while figuring out her next move. As she turned to walk that way, the morning sun glinting off the snow blinded her for a moment. She nearly walked into the tall man who was walking toward her.

"Deanna," he said. "Twice in one week."

Blinking up at him through watery eyes, Deanna realized the tall man was Louis Miller. She was too cold and preoccupied to feel particularly bothered by that fact.

"Oh hi, Lou," she murmured distractedly, She decided she had better grab sunglasses at her place, too; being blinded by snow just wouldn't do if she was to be running from the organization guys.

Louis stared down at her for a moment before saying, "New pajamas?"

"Oh….," she said, looking down at herself as if she was unaware of what she was wearing, "yeah, something like that."

"Look, Deanna, are you okay? I mean, it's freezing out. What the hell are you doing out, dressed like that?" Louis looked genuinely concerned. Deanna would have been crushed by embarrassment at any other time. However, at any other time, she would not have been distracted by the possibility of imminent capture by a secret, magical government organization. As it was, she was trying to look around him and see Main Street, to make sure none of the organization guys were waiting there.

"Yeah, I'm fine," she mumbled. "Just having a rough morning."

As she peered around him, she noticed the robed man she had met the other day standing on the other side of Main Street. He appeared to be staring right at her. When he saw her spot him, he grinned widely and began walking across the street toward her.

"Is there anything I can do?" Louis said quietly. As he spoke, Deanna's eyes were on the robed man. She tried to focus on what Louis was saying, but as the robed man walked across Main Street, several cars drove through him as if he weren't even there. It was very much like when Barb the librarian had walked through Steven; no flash, no sound, the cars just went right through the robed man. She inhaled sharply, causing Lou to turn around and try to spot what she was looking at. He showed no signs of noticing anything out of the ordinary.

"You're not seeing this at all, are you," she said flatly, glancing up at him, then back to the robed man. She already knew the answer to her question.

"Deanna, seriously, how can I help?" Louis put his hand on her arm. She glanced up at him and snorted a humorless laugh.

"I don't know, Lou. I don't even know what day it is," she said with a sigh, her eyes locked on the robed man. He had paused in his approach, and now stood about ten feet away, grinning at her. As she watched, he extended an arm toward her and beckoned her closer.

"March forth," Lou said, encouragingly. Baffled, she looked up at him, trying to figure out if he could now see the robed man. Seeing only concern in his face, she looked back at the robed man, who nodded encouragingly and waved her closer.

"March forth," Lou said again.

Though she didn't understand where his encouraging words were coming from, she chose to believe it was a sign. With no small amount of trepidation, she nodded in response, then walked slowly and uncertainly toward the robed man. It seemed to be her only real option.

Louis

Louis Miller had been on his way to meet with his AA sponsor when he ran into Deanna. Life was largely going well. He had four months sober under his belt since his last relapse. He was feeling good about himself... well, better than he had in a while... and work was going well. A recent press release had garnered some media attention for the bar, and there hadn't been an empty seat in the house for two weeks now.

Sometimes, though, his tendencies toward self-punishment spawned thoughts too loud to ignore, and last night had been one of those times. He had scheduled a meeting with his sponsor this morning so he could talk himself down off the metaphorical ledge.

Seeing Deanna was definitely not on his agenda.

He had no problem with Deanna herself; actually, he liked her very much. However, when she had left the BitterSweet, she had been going through a rough time and things between them had gotten messy. He had been too caught up in his own issues to try to help her deal with hers. He still didn't feel mentally or emotionally able to reach out to her, although the sight of her outdoors in winter in light pajamas definitely raised some concerns in his head.

"Don't say anything, don't get involved," he told himself. "I need to take care of myself. I'm in no position to try and take care of anyone else."

He told himself that, over and over, but Deanna's bizarrely erratic behavior was really getting to him. She was barely even making eye contact; she kept looking around him, wide eyed, toward Main Street. When he glanced to see what she was looking at, he saw nothing of interest — just the usual Main Street activity. His mild concern for her mental state was starting to become full blown alarm.

He found himself asking her if there was any way he could be of help to her, even as he cursed himself for being stupid enough to utter the words. "I am NOT in a position to help her, dammit," he thought. He felt relieved that she ignored his question, but certainly not reassured about her well-being when she said, expressionlessly, "You're not seeing any of this, are you." It was as if she were acknowledging that she may be hallucinating, and seemed quite used to it. Lou found himself biting his lip; he really wished he were in a better place, mentally, and that he knew just the right thing to say.

94

"Deanna, seriously, how can I help?" he found his mouth blurting as his mind cursed it for doing so.

"I don't know, Lou. I don't even know what day it is," she answered, her eyes fixed on an apparently arbitrary spot in the air behind him.

He felt a moment's relief. That, at least, he could help with. "It's March fourth," he said.

She looked at him as if he had just uttered a spell in Sanskrit and whispered, "What?"

"It's....March.....fourth," he repeated, slowly, then watched as she stumbled past him toward Main Street. He watched her walk toward the road, momentarily concerned that she was going to walk out into traffic. Then, suddenly, she was gone.

He figured he must have blinked and missed her turning the corner. He dearly hoped she would be alright. He wished he could run after her and say just the right thing to help her get it together.

As it was, though, he turned on his heel and walked away, as fast as he could. He really needed to talk to someone, and his sponsor was waiting.

Steven

He sat in the tiny cell that had been designed for Deanna, staring at his reflection in the glass, wondering how he had gotten there.

A nagging voice in the back of his mind said he should have listened to his doubts about Larsen's plan to break Deanna down and wipe away part of her brain. Some voice inside of Steven had said that it was the wrong thing to do, but he had of course ignored it. He knew better than to question orders. His orders always upheld the greater good, even when he didn't understand them.

He knew in the core of his soul that that was the case. He was not, after all, a bad person. He had never done anything really WRONG. He had always just done the best he could with what life gave him. Life had given him the organization, and everything became so much easier. He had a purpose, and that purpose was to uphold the greater good. All he had to do in order to fulfill that purpose was to follow his superior's orders, and those orders had been to bring Deanna breakfast and be nice to her.

Since that was the case – that he had been following orders, and his orders upheld the greater good – answering the question, "How did I get here?" was pretty easy: he had gotten there because Deanna was a bitch.

She had used her feminine wiles, and such. She had made a fool of him.

Larsen had been right to treat her like he had, and to want to wipe her brain. Clearly, she was a terrible person.

As he let his anger grow, he realized how comforting it was. Being angry at Deanna alleviated his fears about Larsen's imminent reaction to the situation, and any doubts he had about their role in causing her to flee. It all seemed so simple, now.

Deanna was a bad person.

He, Steven, had just been following orders.

The orders he followed had been intended to make the world, and in fact Deanna herself, better.

None of this, then, was his fault.

He breathed a sigh of relief, and tried to figure out how to explain that to Larsen.

Deanna

As Deanna walked toward the robed man, he kept his arm extended toward her. She found her own arm extending, almost involuntarily, and when she was close enough to him, she took hold of his hand.

The second she did so, she felt a shift. She was warmer, for one thing. Everything around her looked the same, but something *felt* different.

She looked up at his face, and he smiled. "My queen," he murmured.

"Who are you?"

His grin broadened. "No one, really."

"Why do you refer to me as 'my queen'?"

"Are you not royalty?"

She chuckled. "Um, no. Can't say I am."

"Why can't you say it?"

"No, I meant... I'm not royalty."

"Oh, I see." His eyes twinkled with amusement, as if he were placating a child.

Cars rushed past them, and the occasional pedestrian scurried by, bundled against the cold. No one seemed to notice them. She felt as if they were in their own little bubble of warmth and privacy, not out of the world but not affected by it, either. She could still hear the sounds around them – at that very moment, Tom Petty's "You Don't Know How it Feels" was beginning to play on Main Street's speakers, and a teenager scurrying past them was screaming for his friends to wait up – but it all seemed somehow far away.

"Are you one of them? Are you part of the organization?" she asked.

Again, he looked amused, and shook his head. "I am part of the ultimate organization, and no organization at all. I am order in chaos, and chaos in structure. But mostly, I am connection."

"To what?"

"What do you believe?"

She stared up at him quizzically, feeling as if she were talking to the Cheshire Cat from Alice in Wonderland, or possibly the Mad Hatter. "I don't know," she finally answered.

"Perhaps it is time to give it some thought," he answered gently.

Deanna did not know what to make of this strange man, yet his presence was strangely, inexplicably comforting. Reassuring. She felt like everything was going to be alright – better than alright – while she held his hand. She stared up at him with an overwhelming blend of wonder, awe, and confusion. She had a million questions, but didn't know which to ask.

He must have sensed her mental turmoil, because he squeezed her hand gently and said, "Let's take a walk," then gently led her down Main Street.

As they walked, he seemed to study each person they passed, unnoticed. He paused at store windows and peered inside with great interest. No one showed any reaction to his scrutiny; Deanna wondered if they were invisible to everyone else, like Steven had been. It was a strange feeling.

After they had walked a block or two, the robed man began to speak.

"You have been taught a bit about your galaxy, I assume. The way all of the planets orbit the sun. Different planets, different orbits, same sun."

Deanna nodded.

"People are much the same. Each is their own world, but they all orbit the same sun."

She thought for a moment. "Who or what is that sun?"

"That goes back to what you believe. How you perceive it, in your own world, dictates what it is in your world."

"Are you talking about God?"

He bowed his head slightly to the side. "Broadly speaking, yes. But also, no."

"Are you trying to tell me I am walking down Main Street with some kind of personification of a connection to God?"

"Broadly speaking, yes. But also, no," he repeated, laughing. "It's not that straightforward, my lady. I have met people while they were in prayer, or meditation. I have also met people while they were consumed with inspiration, or passion, or motivation. I meet people in all sorts of circumstances, when they awaken to the divine spark inside every moment and molecule of their existence. What I explain as being the sun to your worlds could be called God, or Love, or the Divine... None of those would be entirely right or wrong. It is difficult to put labels on such things."

"But...I don't really think connection to such things comes in person form," she said.

"Then I'm someone else," he said, quite agreeably.

"I mean.... You can't be a connection to the Divine and a person. Can you?"

"Do you think I am?"

"I don't know," she admitted, sighing. "I'm not really understanding any of this."

"It's quite simple, my lady. It's as simple as you allow it to be."

She sighed again. "I've finally lost my mind completely, haven't I?"

"If that is what you choose to accept, my lady, that can be the answer."

She shook her head.

"If that is not what you choose to accept, then, it is time for you to release that notion and accept something else."

"I want to..." Deanna trailed off for a moment. "I just don't know how, I guess."

"Just allow it to be, my lady."

"I wish it was that simple..."

"It IS. Just allow it to be. Allow yourself to be queen of your world. Allow yourself to know the answers you seek. Allow reality to be what it is. Allow yourself to be responsible for your world and your experience. Allow, lady, just allow and it shall be."

They strolled down Main Street aimlessly, in silence.

Then the robed man said thoughtfully, "My lady, you are responsible for every single thing that you experience. I realize that thought frightens many people, but it will help you to accept that."

"You mean I'm responsible for myself being kidnapped by a secret government organization that wants to brainwash me or something? Because I think that was an accident." Her response was defensive, and dripping with a bit more sarcasm than she had meant it to.

"There are no accidents," he replied warmly, unaffected by her tone. "You had a need to confront some personal demons before you could become queen of your world. Those demons were given to you."

She considered his words.

"Are you saying.... Wait, what are you saying? Did I somehow create those men and their organization?"

He chuckled. "No, my lady, you did not create them. They exist, independently of you. But when worlds collide, they fit into each other as they can. Perhaps your world needed the threat of being eradicated in order for you to embrace your power. Did you not tell me, just a few hours ago, that you are capable of handling anything? That you are safe and free? You so rarely say such things."

She looked up at him, shocked. "That's what I was saying last night. My affirmations. When I was meditating. But I was alone."

"You're never alone, my lady, when you seek me."

She was beginning to believe the truth of what he said, of who he was. She wanted to ask him everything, every question she had ever had about life. "But why... how... if we are all in charge of our own worlds, why would anyone choose to be... to be bad? Did I somehow make the General be a bad guy?"

"Yes and no, my Queen," he responded, laughing again. "Those men are not necessarily 'bad guys,' as you put it. No one sets out to be a 'bad guy.' But different worlds have different effects on each other's orbits. Sometimes worlds collide, and fit into each other in any way they can. Sometimes people never truly take control of their worlds, and they become moons, trailing in the orbit of other worlds without responsibility. The answers may be as simple as you allow, but they are also not black and white issues."

She gazed at him for a few beats before saying, "I don't think I have a clue what all that meant, but I hope I'll figure it out."

He laughed uproariously, and she giggled in response.

"In time, you will understand all," he assured her.

She thought of another question. "What about the Rasta... David Carver? What about him? How does he fit in to all this?"

The robed man closed his eyes for a second, and a flicker of sadness passed over his face. "Such a gifted individual, so blessed. More than many. It hurt so very deeply to watch as he lost sight of his connection. Once he did, he cut himself off from everything and everyone, and he became isolated, alone. Just his ego and his work. And his work, shall we say, had repercussions for a man with no connections in his world."

"He lost sight of his... connection," Deanna repeated slowly.

He boomed laughter in response. "I never lost sight of him, though!"

Something about the robed man's explanation of Carver made Deanna think of her dream, and the tiny sun over the statue that had become her. Was it a warning of some kind?

"But... you're saying I am queen of my world, or I should be. Wouldn't that make me no different than him? Ego-driven?"

He smiled and shook his head. "No, my Lady, there is a balance. You must understand you are responsible for all that you experience, but there is another force working with you. Let's call it the great mystery. It responds to you, and your connection to it makes you stronger." He paused and considered his next words. "One might say that you have been the polar opposite of your Rasta Man for most of your life. Always seeking connection, never acknowledging that you have the power to rule your world. Perhaps that opposite polarity created a vacuum that drew him to you. Perhaps your destinies are intertwined, and he was meant to find his way to your world so that you can save each other. Perhaps your two worlds collided to form a new world, a better world." He paused, and grinned. "Or, perhaps you are just insane, and he is just a crazy, homeless man, and this is all in your head."

She searched his face for answers, but saw only the benevolent amusement that seemed to radiate from him at all times. "Do you know?" she asked him. "Do you know which it is? Do you know what's real and what isn't?"

"YES," he answered emphatically. "I know that it all depends."

"On what?"

"On what YOU know, my Queen," he said, resting a hand on top of her head.

"I'm not sure if you're the most ambiguous person I've ever met, or if everything is just simpler than it seems. Or both."

Again, the wide, infectious grin flashed. "Definitely both, my Queen. Whenever there are two possibilities, the answer is always 'both.'"

Deanna found herself chuckling and shaking her head, though she could not really explain her amusement. She just felt so... happy, walking down the street with him.

"Do you have a name?" she asked. "I feel like I should be able to call you something."

"You just did," he said. "You described me as 'You,' and we both knew you meant me. You may continue to call me 'You.' It will suffice."

She giggled. "That's not really a name."

"I'm not really a person, so it fits for now," he answered lightly. "Perhaps, in time, we will figure out another name for me."

She looked at him, then, with a long, considering, appraising look. "You're not, are you? You're not a person. You're really some kind of divine connection. This is real. This isn't just me being crazy."

As she stared at him, she noticed his robes looked less like the bedsheets she had originally taken them to be, and more like fine silk. The staff she had thought was a fallen tree branch was actually carved with intricate symbols and seemed to pulse with energy. He looked more like a mystical being than like the homeless man she had originally taken him to be.

The robed man... You... glanced down at himself and grinned. His eyes closed for a moment in apparent ecstasy over the transformation of his clothing. "Ahhh," he murmured. "The lady begins to understand."

She returned his grin. She still really didn't understand everything You said, but she was beginning to accept that he was real, and that she was not insane. If that was the case, she might also have to accept that he was right about her being responsible for her own experience, and queen of her world.

It was a good feeling, that acceptance.

David

David rode his motorcycle down the long stretch of road, enjoying the feeling of the ocean breeze on his skin. He felt more alive, more aware then he had in a long, long time.

After a while, though, he became aware of a feeling that something was missing. He could not put his finger on it, but something just didn't feel right. This glorious ride felt... incomplete. Almost... false.

He pulled over, onto the beach, and sat on his idling motorcycle, staring at the waves. Something stirred in his memory, and he tried to identify it. He stared vacantly at the waves crashing to the shore, willing the memories to identify themselves.

After a time, he lifted his gaze to the horizon. He watched that quiet place where the ocean met the sky for a long while, not thinking, just observing.

Somewhere in the tangled web that was left of his mind, something clicked, and he said aloud, "Damn."

He suddenly realized that this place, this motorcycle, as lovely as they were, were not his. They were not, in the truest sense of the word, real.

He got off his motorcycle and walked toward the ocean, wondering how to get to another place, a more real place. He had found himself in new places all the time, without control, for a very long time. This time was different, though. This time, he wanted to go to a specific place; he wanted to go to HIS place, wherever that may be. He wanted to intentionally walk between worlds, rather than being thrown around like a leaf on the wind. He needed to find some connection between this place and his own place, his own home, even though he could not remember where that home was or what it was like.

As he walked toward the ocean, he noticed a long sandbar that extended, just under the water, for as far as he could see. It seemed to present itself as the best option for his next path, so he took off his worn, tattered shoes, and walked out onto the sandbar.

After he took a few steps, he suddenly flashed to a scene in which he was looking up at a tall man who looked lovingly at him and said, "You are always safe, my Queen.... As long as you choose to be."

Just as suddenly as it came, the image disappeared. David fell down on the sandbar, disoriented. Then, he gazed out at the horizon, picked himself up, and marched onward.

He didn't know what he had just seen or who the man had been, but he knew he had to find him. He knew the man hadn't been behind him, on the road, so he must be somewhere ahead. Grasping that thought, the most solid certainty he had felt in many, many years, David marched forward with a sense of determination he had not thought it was possible to feel at this stage in his life.

Deanna

They walked toward her apartment in companionable silence. Deanna felt more lighthearted than she had in quite some time.

When they reached her apartment, though, she felt a moment's panic. "What's going to happen now?"

"Whatever you like, my lady."

"You're going to go away, though?"

He smiled and shook his head. "Only in this form. You can always find me if you reach inside."

She bit her lip, nervously. "I don't want you to go. I feel safe with you."

"You are always safe, my Queen... as long as you choose to be."

She smiled despite herself, nodded, and said, "I had a feeling you'd say something like that."

He shrugged. "I only speak the truth," he said, then bent over and kissed her forehead. She felt his warm lips press against her head, and then, in an instant, he vanished.

And she was alone again.

Realizing time was of the essence, she ran into her apartment and put on the warmest sweater she could find, with jeans, several pairs of socks, and boots. She put her warmest winter coat over all of that, with a hat, a scarf, and gloves. She looked around for her phone, to no avail, but found a pack of cigarettes, which made her happy. She grabbed her wallet, purse, and sunglasses, then ran back outside, and down the street, with no real idea of where she was going. She was just going AWAY, away from anywhere she thought Steven and Larsen would look first. Despite the comforting words of the robed man, she did not yet feel ready to face them; she did not feel confident in her ability to take control of the situation.

After she ran a few blocks, she sat down on an arbitrary bench and lit a cigarette while she tried to collect her thoughts and form a plan. She knew she should keep moving, but at the same time – why? To go where? They would be able to find her anywhere, wouldn't they?

"And yet," she thought, "they can't seem to find the Rasta Man."

That thought, at least, was encouraging. If they couldn't find him, maybe, just maybe, they wouldn't be able to find her, either. Maybe, if she could figure out why the chance encounters she had had with him were important, she could figure out how to get them off her back.

The last time she had thought about the Rasta Man, before all of this mess, was at the laundromat. She had pictured him riding his motorcycle down a highway someplace warm and beautiful, and the thought had made her smile. Even now, as she sat on the bench, she smiled at the mental picture.

"The last place I really saw him, then, was in my imagination," she thought.

It was an intriguing notion. A day ago, she would have thought nothing of it, but she had just taken a stroll down the street with some kind of embodiment of connection. Anything, it seemed, was possible.

"And I'm the queen of my world," she murmured. Then, she closed her eyes and began to release her thoughts, embracing her connection to the divine, as she endeavored to return to that memory.

Eric

Eric sat in front of four separate monitors, studying them all as data scrolled past.

As John walked by, he glanced at the monitors and said, "Well, she's gone, did you happen to notice that while you were examining her molecules and whatnot?"

"Of course," Eric murmured. "I think she's back in Woodford, but she kind of disappeared once she got there."

"Don't you think you should tell your buddy the General what's going on?"

Eric paused and glanced at John before answering, "I'm not sure."

"I mean….he's gonna know soon, anyway. Get the brownie points, bro."

"I'm…. not sure," Eric repeated.

"Oh, what," John said casually, "you mean because of how he's turning all evil about this waitress chick?"

"You've thought so, too?" Eric's voice sounded grateful.

"I mean, yeah, bro. I watched some of his 'interviews' with her. And now he wants to erase her brain? What the fuck is that shit?"

"I've been really perplexed by his reasoning," Eric blurted, relieved to get it off his chest. "I understand he wants to find Carver, but this is… odd."

"Odd? I was considering buying him a Darth Vader mask to accessorize his turn to the dark side."

Eric snickered, then frowned. "I was kind of hoping it was just me."

"Nah, bro. Anyway, how did she 'kind of' disappear once she got back to Woodford?"

"Don't really know. She was there, then she wasn't."

"Maybe there's something funky going on in that town. Carver was there, Steven found her there, and Larsen started going all evil…. Weird stuff, for sure," John observed.

"Yeah. I….." Eric trailed off and stared at his shoes.

"Did you have something to add to that, or was 'I' really your main, take home point there?" John asked drily, after waiting fruitlessly for Eric to finish his sentence.

"I might have… there could… I thought maybe I saw…." Eric stammered, then trailed off again.

"I have no idea where you're going with this, bro, but I'm riveted. Let me know when you think you can make it to the end of the sentence."

"I-think-I-saw-Carver's-energy-signature-in-the-waitress's-molecular-scan-yesterday," Eric told his shoes in one long breath.

"Like…wait. Like, her energy output is the same as his?"

"No, hers was hers, and her molecules were all normal, but his energy might have been flickering around in her molecular structure for a second."

"Did you actually smoke crack before this happened?"

Eric snickered in response, then shook his head.

"I don't know what that could even mean, bro," John said, incredulously. "I feel like we have to tell the General, 'cause I just have no clue."

"Yeah, but… I'm not sure," Eric repeated, hesitantly.

"Right, the evil." John sat down heavily in a chair next to Eric and stared vacantly at the monitors, then said, "Well, shit."

Eric nodded morosely, and the two of them sat quietly in their confusion, watching a never-ending stream of apparently useless data scroll by on the monitors.

"We're gonna have to strategize a bit before we talk to the General," John said, and Eric, having nothing else to say, stared at his shoes.

Steven

Once Steven had spent what seemed like a fairly long time marinating in his anger, the door to the cell opened, and General Larsen entered, whistling. When he saw Steven sitting alone on the cot, his whistle ended abruptly.

"She stole my Broom," Steven explained, flatly.

"Oh, dear," Larsen answered, with feeling. "How did she know how to use it?"

"Because you really just have to push a button?"

"But the focus, the direction... she couldn't know how to REALLY use it. Odds are, she's back in Woodford. That's the only place her little mind would have been thinking of. Chin up, boy, we'll find her."

Steven nodded mutely, his mind still occupied by the many ways in which Deanna was clearly a bad person.

Larsen pulled out his Wand and tapped away at the screen for a moment. Suddenly, he paused and looked up sharply. "Why didn't you use your Wand to brief me before I came in here?"

Steven blinked in surprise. "Honestly, sir, I was so mad I didn't even think about it."

"I see. And how long did you sit here, being 'mad'?"

"I'm not really sure. Twenty minutes? Thirty?"

"I see. So, for roughly half an hour, Miss Flanagan has been on the run and neither you nor the techs felt the need to make me aware of the situation."

Steven's knee began to shake. "Well...yes, sir, I suppose that's true."

"Does that seem like it was the best course of action, in retrospect?"

"No, sir. I suppose I let my anger overrule my sense of logic."

"Indeed. Well, let's go see what John and Eric's excuse is."

They left the cell and walked through the empty testing room, down the hall to John and Eric's private lab, which was a fairly chaotic room full of computers and devices in various stages of development. There were a few band posters on the walls that John had hung, which, in combination with the general mess, gave the little room a similar ambience to the bedroom of a fourteen year old emo boy.

Whenever Steven had previously visited the techs' lab, he had found Eric working at one computer and John sitting across from him, more often than not playing video games or listening to music. This was not the case today. The two techs sat side by side in front of a computer that had four monitors set up, with data scrolling down each one. Neither of them were looking at the monitors, though. They both stared at Steven and Larsen. Eric wore a look that could only be described as fear, whereas John had an air of forced nonchalance.

"Oh, hey, guys," John greeted them casually.

Although Steven sensed there was something going on with the techs, he felt it would be better to stay quiet and let Larsen take the lead. After all, if he had alerted Larsen to the situation as soon as it occurred, everything would probably be made right by now.

"Gentlemen. I assume you're aware that Miss Flanagan has left us?"

"Yes, sir, we know she's back in Woodford maybe but she keeps disappearing," Eric quickly mumbled to his shoes.

"And did you think at any point that it might be a good idea to alert me to this situation?"

Nobody said a word. The silence was so heavy, Steven thought it could be described as crushing.

"Gentlemen, that was a question. Which implies that it requires an answer."

John and Eric glanced at each other, then Eric looked back to his shoes, apparently for their wise counsel. Steven had never felt so awkward on someone else's behalf. He was therefore relieved when John started talking, though his relief died out quickly when he understood what the tech was saying.

"Well, the thing is, General... the thing is... you know when Anakin kills all those kids in those godawful new Star Wars movies, and it doesn't make any sense? Like, he thinks the Jedi are corrupt and he has to protect his wife and kid, but then he just randomly kills a bunch of kids, and you're kind of like, what the fuck? It's kind of like this waitress chick is your bunch of little kids."

There was a moment's silence as everyone attempted to process this, then Eric told his shoes, "We want to be taken off this assignment, sir."

"I see," Larsen said coldly. "Because of a movie?"

"No sir," Eric said, finally looking up from his shoes and staring the General in the eye. "Because of you."

"Yeah dude, it's getting, just, like, uncomfortable," John explained. "I'm not really sure where you're going with this whole brain-erasing business, but I feel like you should just leave this chick alone."

Standing behind the General, Steven could not see the man's face. He was fairly glad about that, just at that moment. He could almost feel icy waves of anger emanating from his commanding officer.

"I see," Larsen said quietly, then turned slowly to look at Steven. "And you, Drisbane? Do you feel the same way?"

"I...no...of course not, sir." As he said the words, he honestly hoped he was telling the truth. "I would never question your orders."

The General nodded once, then turned back to the techs. "You do understand that if you're removed from this assignment, all memory of it will have to be taken away from you."

There was a pause as the techs glanced at each other, then nervously, unexpectedly broke into laughter.

"What, exactly, is comical about that?" Larsen asked, his voice sharp.

"Well, you see," John explained, "you'd kind of need us to design the equipment for the procedure. And we're not going to do that."

As the general opened his mouth to respond, Eric picked up what looked like a souped-up Broom. The round, black button was the same, but it was on a much longer base. He held it up and mumbled, "We made this instead."

"And what, pray tell, is that?"

"Insurance," Eric said, and pushed the button.

Every device the techs had made, from the jumbled heaps of wires around the room to the Wand in Larsen's hand, vanished. Steven looked around, aghast, then experimentally felt in the pocket where he kept his SmartWand; it, too, was gone. He glanced at Larsen and saw only seething rage. He decided he had to act to diffuse the situation.

"Guys. Listen," he began. "There's gotta be a way we can work this out. Compromise."

John snickered. "Doesn't feel so great, being at someone else's mercy with no real control, does it? Welcome to our world."

"You've never been at anyone's mercy," Steven protested. "You're our coworkers. You do your job, and we appreciate you."

"Listen, navy boy," John continued, "maybe you think this shit is okay, but nobody is wiping any part of my mind away just so I can be off the assignment of torturing a waitress. This is not what I signed on for."

"We just wanted to find Carver," Eric interjected quietly.

"Precisely, Eric. That's what we came to this organization for. When we learned about David Carver, we wanted to find him and fix him and pick his brain. We left fucking NASA because we thought we could

111

learn more here. Wiping away people's brains was not part of the deal. We just wanted to learn more about magic."

"Guys, come on. We're still trying to find Carver, but this woman has turned up, and could be connected to him," Steven said, as soothingly as he could. "That's the only reason for all this."

"Really?" John's voice was about four octaves higher than usual. "You're really gonna stick with that?" He gestured toward Larsen and squeaked, "He just berated her and abused her for how fucking long, because Carver? Are you actually brainwashed, man? Did he get to you first?"

"I'm not brainwashed," Steven snapped back, before pausing and trying to reel his anger in. He took a deep breath. "Look, even if you don't approve of the methods we've been using or the reasoning behind this assignment, she has now stolen organization technology. She has my Broom. We can't allow that to go on."

Eric brandished his own, Broomlike device and mumbled, "Not anymore."

There was a momentary hush throughout the room as that statement sunk in for everyone present. Larsen broke the silence. "Gentlemen, where has all of the equipment gone?"

"Someplace safe," John said, "where it will stay until we've had a little talk and worked on some issues;"

"What sort of issues?" Larsen's voice had become so icy, Steven thought he might actually feel colder upon hearing it.

"Well, for one, when did we become bad guys? How is kidnapping waitresses and brainwashing them going to help us find Carver?" John's voice sounded more agitated than Steven had ever heard him.

"Why are you so certain she's connected to him?" Eric asked quietly.

Larsen heaved a sigh. "We've been over this. There is no such thing as coincidence. She somehow, by accident, managed to meet him, then Drisbane found her. Her ability to see through his shields is an obvious red flag. There's something going on with that woman, and we need to get to the bottom of it. She met him!" He yelled the last part loudly enough to make all three of the other men jump. "She met him, when we've been searching for him for eighteen years!"

"I've only been working on this assignment for like a year, bro," John acerbically observed. Steven shushed him.

Larsen continued as if he hadn't noticed the interruption. "There must be something about her, something we've missed. There's no other explanation. I've been looking for Dave – for Carver, I mean – for so long! How could this ...this ...stranger be allowed to find him? What possible quality does she have that I lack? I've been LOOKING FOR HIM FOR EIGHTEEN YEARS!" His voice rose, and cracked, and Steven was horrified to realize he had begun to sob. "It's just not fair," Larsen sounded like a four year old having a tantrum. "It's just not fair."

Awkward silence prevailed for a long moment before Eric ventured, "I don't really think that's a good reason for wiping away people's brains."

The General gave no response except continued sobbing, so Steven responded for him. "Everything else aside, there must be some connection. Not only did she meet him, several times, but she could see me when I was fully cloaked. How do you explain that, unless we consider the possibility that Carver did something to her? Do you have some other explanation?"

John and Eric glanced at each other, and Eric shrugged almost imperceptibly before looking back to his shoes. John spread his hands and suggested brightly, "The Lord works in mysterious ways?"

"There's got to be more to it than that."

Eric and John glanced at each other, and Steven thought he detected a sense of alarm in that glance. He wondered what the techs were hiding.

"Even if that's true, there must be a better way to get to the bottom of things," John finally answered. "We haven't even got anyone from the Boogie Man Patrol working on this assignment to prevent the energy's negative backlash. Do you really want to use the energy with negative intentions? Can't you imagine what that could bring back on us?"

"Well... but...," the General was still weeping, and uncharacteristically flustered. "If all the extra nonsense is wiped from her brain, maybe it will show us the truth that she's hiding. Maybe it will show us how she fits in to all of this. That's not negative intention, it's furthering our mission. We are meant to bring Carver in by any means necessary, and the end justifies the means in this case."

"I doubt she would think so," Eric murmured.

"It would help her, too, Eric," Steven stepped in again. "The General has discovered that she has some pretty serious issues, mentally. This would give her a fresh start."

The techs glanced at one another once more, then John said drily, "I really don't think it's up to us to decide who's got issues we should wipe away. Larsen's over there crying his eyes out because he's jealous this lady got to see his friend and he couldn't. You," he addressed Steven, "can't seem to have an original thought unless someone tells you to. Eric has the social skills of an agoraphobic mole. And I…. well, I just don't think we are in any position to be judging whether or not to wipe away part of someone's brain."

A snarky response was forming on Steven's lips, but it was chased away by surprise when Larsen whispered, "You're absolutely right."

"He…what?" Steven asked.

"He's completely right." The General's voice was hushed and thick with tears. "I've been going about this all wrong. I've let my emotions get the better of me. I should have been trying to get her to work with us voluntarily, rather than forcing my will on her. Carver himself would be ashamed of me." He wiped away his tears and clapped John on the shoulder. "Thank you, boys. Both of you. It took an incredible courage to make me see I've been wrong, and I am incredibly grateful to you both."

Both John and Eric shrugged, and John said, "It's all good, man."

Steven felt overwhelmingly confused, and more than a little angry. All he had been doing was following Larsen's orders, and now the General had not only reversed his position completely, but expressed gratitude to the techs for rebelling against his original stance. It was maddening, baffling, and unbelievably frustrating.

He had no idea how to react, so he stayed silent for as long as he could.

David

He had been walking along the sandbar for as long as he could remember, now, which truthfully wasn't very long at all. However, he remembered why he was walking, and that was an improvement on things. For so long, he had wandered with no idea of why, how, or where he was going. At least now he knew: he was looking for someplace real. He was looking for where he belonged. He was looking for the man in his vision, who he was pretty sure could help him, though he didn't know why he thought that.

As he walked, he murmured, "Use my gifts. Find a world where I can be safe. Find you again." At least, he murmured the closest approximation of those words that he could muster.

Although the sun shone brightly, it was not terribly hot. He waded through the shallow water that occasionally flowed over the sandbar, or he walked on the sand when it did not, without feeling hot, or tired, or really much of anything at all. He simply walked, almost oblivious to his surroundings. None of it seemed real. He just wanted something real.

This went on and on, an unchanging blur of sun and water and sand, until suddenly he saw a flash of light in his periphery. He paused and looked around; for a moment, but saw no change in the scenery. Then, as he began to walk forward again, he saw a woman standing about twenty yards ahead of him. She was looking around with an air of apparent interest. When she noticed him, she smiled and waved. He smiled and waved back, almost against his will.

There was something familiar about her. He walked closer, unafraid and unperturbed by her sudden, inexplicable presence.

"Hi there," she called as he walked closer.

He nodded wordlessly in response, unable to remember what one says in such situations.

"Are you... are you David Carver?" she stammered.

He thought very hard about that. He knew those words, they definitely sounded very familiar. Although he wasn't one hundred percent sure, he nodded. He was pretty sure he might be that thing she had said.

"I'm Deanna. Do you remember me at all?"

He stared at her for a few seconds, then shrugged.

"I used to… you used to… sometimes I gave you cigarettes. Before. When I worked at the BitterSweet Bistro in Woodford. Do you remember?"

He considered her words. Many of them did not make sense to him, but he felt like they should, somehow. They conjured images in his mind of a crowded street and of an empty, dimly lit room filled with tables and stools, with this lady in both places. He remembered trying to tell her how he had found himself there, even though he did not really recall himself, and he remembered that she was nice to him. He remembered she told him he could be safe in her strange world. All of these things appeared as vague images in his mind; for no logical reason, he simply felt safe with this woman.

He thought all this, and he nodded slowly. "Nice lady," he offered.

She grinned and nodded. "Yes, you called me that once or twice. I'm glad you remember. I think maybe we can help each other."

He cocked his head to the side and looked at her quizzically. He couldn't figure out what it was about her that he found so reassuring. He felt like he understood her, and vice versa, even if he didn't fully understand what she was saying. A voice in his memory whispered: "You know very little, right now. But you did know many things. You knew the cause and solution to the problem you're having now. You knew what was important in life. You knew me. You knew you weren't alone."

He wasn't sure where those words came from or who had said them, but he was pretty sure they were important. "Not alone," he murmured in his hoarse voice.

"That's right, you're not alone," she answered. "I'm here now, and You is always with you, even when you don't know it." She giggled. "That sounds funny, when I say it like that. He told me to call him 'You,' but maybe you don't know him by that? He's a very tall man who wears robes. I think maybe you knew him, once."

David's brow furrowed slightly as he tried to figure out what she was saying, and he said nothing. It felt like something in his brain was jiggling as he listened to her speak. It was not necessarily an unpleasant sensation, but an odd one. He didn't know what to make of it. He jiggled his head a bit to see if it would stop the feeling; it didn't. He waved his hand to encourage her to talk more, so that he could explore the feeling further. She looked at him quizzically, as if she didn't understand the request. He waved again and, after searching his mind thoroughly for the right words, said, "More."

"You mean... do you mean more of a description?"

He shrugged and nodded.

"Well, he's very, very tall. Maybe six and a half feet tall. And he has dreadlocks that go to his shoulders, and a cocoa complexion. He carries a staff, and he wears sandals. He, um. He's not actually a person. He's a connection to the Divine, or something. It's all a bit confusing. But I think maybe I need to help you find him."

Maybe it wasn't actually his brain jiggling. Maybe it was something IN his brain. A thought? A memory? Maybe it was waking up. Maybe it was dancing. He was pretty sure thoughts didn't dance like that, though. Whatever the case, it felt weird, so he took up the metaphorical security blanket of repeating his mantra. "Use my gifts. Find a world where I can be safe. Find you again."

After he had repeated it several times, he realized she was listening intently and even watching his lips move, as if she were trying very hard to understand him. People didn't usually do that. Lots of new things happening.

"Yes!" she suddenly exclaimed, delightedly. "You need to find You again! That's exactly right!"

He stopped talking and smiled with her. He liked smiling, he hadn't done much of it in a long time. It felt nice.

"Do you actually have any idea what I'm talking about?" she asked.

He shrugged, still smiling.

She sighed. "Okay, we need to figure this out." She looked around, then said, "Do you know where we are?"

He looked around, too. Then he said, "Not mine."

She nodded. "I think we're in my mind, actually. Which doesn't make a whole lot of sense, but it seems to be true. And I think... I think we can help each other, but I'm not sure how, really. I need to become queen of my world, apparently, and I think I have to help you regain your connection to... to... to You. And to your world." She paused and contemplated their surroundings for a moment. "When I met him, he told me that sometimes worlds collide, and fit into each other in any way they can. I think your world is stuck in my world, right now."

He nodded, staring at the sky. "Motorcycle," he offered. That was all he really remembered of his world.

"Yes," she sighed again. "I wonder if the organization knows where your brand new motorcycle is. Those men...Steven Drisbane and Benjamin Larsen. Do you know them?"

He blinked. There was something familiar in those words. "Bed?" He shook his head; that wasn't right. "Ben," he corrected himself.

"You do know them," she murmured. "Maybe that could help."

They sat in companionable silence for a few moments. He closed his eyes for a moment, and the vision he had had before he started walking the sandbar flashed in his mind.

"Always safe, my lady, as long as you choose to be," he intoned, repeating the words of the man in his vision. He opened his eyes again and saw that the nice lady was looking at him with big eyes and an open mouth; she was surprised. He didn't know why.

"Can you do me a favor, David?" she asked once she had gotten over her surprise. She took his hand in hers, and said, "Let's both just close our eyes and clear our minds, and be open to connection."

He shrugged. She put her free hand over his eyes and said, "Close your eyes." He obeyed.

They sat like that for a long while, holding each other's hands with their eyes closed and their minds open. After a bit, he felt a hand on his head and opened his eyes, expecting to see the nice lady.

"Hello, old friend," the robed man said, smiling fondly at him.

"Find you again!" he exclaimed, happily.

"All you ever had to do was look," You said, and offered David a hand to help him up.

Benjamin

He was incredibly embarrassed about the fact that he couldn't seem to stop crying, but there was no help for it. It was as if all of the emotions he had pushed aside for eighteen years had finally broken through some dam and were now leaking out of his eyes.

He tried to wipe away his tears as he said, "Thank you, boys. Both of you. It took an incredible courage to make me see I've been wrong, and I am incredibly grateful to you both."

The techs seemed as embarrassed by his gratitude as he felt about his own tears, so he switched tactics. "So now what?" he asked. "I am open to your advice, gentlemen."

Eric and John glanced at each other, then Eric quickly mumbled, "I think we should still find her, just not wipe her brain."

"She... she might be helpful to our investigation, you're not wrong about that," John admitted.

Drisbane sounded rather irate as he asked, "What makes you say that?" Benjamin couldn't imagine why the boy seemed bent out of shape.

John only shrugged, and glanced at Eric again. Eric mumbled something Benjamin couldn't hear. Apparently, neither could Drisbane, who snapped with great vitriol, "What the hell did you say?"

"Drisbane!" Benjamin exclaimed. "What in God's name has come over you, boy?"

The boy turned his icy stare toward him. "What's come over ME? You've suddenly decided that everything we've been doing is wrong. You're thanking these guys and asking their advice because they basically staged a rebellion. And you want to know what's come over ME?"

"Ensign ..."

"That's right, sir, I AM an Ensign. I'm an officer in this organization and I have followed every order you've given me, and I have ALWAYS performed to the best of my abilities, no matter what thankless task you've given me. And have you ever thanked me? No. But you thank these two for flat out disobedience."

"You just have your panties in a bunch because I said you don't have any original thoughts," John observed.

If looks really could kill, John would have died in that moment.

"Gentlemen, please," Benjamin began. His tears were subsiding, and the calm of catharsis was all he felt in that moment. "This is completely unnecessary. Drisbane, I'm sorry if you feel invalidated. You are a good operative. I rely on you heavily. But what these boys did for me..." he trailed off for a moment and rubbed his eyes. "For so long, I've just been reacting to circumstances. Burying my feelings and reacting. It's a sad state of affairs. You know why I admired Carver so much? Well, many reasons, but one was that he always took charge of his own destiny. He was a natural born leader. No one even believed in magic, but he isolated the energy and developed tools to make it accessible to us. He... nothing could stop him. He was amazing." He paused and rubbed his eyes again, then looked intently at Drisbane. "You and I, boy... we haven't been so amazing. We've been reactive, passive. Rather than taking charge of our lives, our mission, we've been reacting to whatever gets thrown our way. It's sad. I'm ashamed of myself, and I want better for you. I realize that now. I realize it because John and Eric took charge of the situation and showed me how terribly I was behaving. They had the courage to stand up to me and remind me of what's important.

"I... I've been so blind. I've been burying my feelings and rationalizing my behaviors, just so I could spare myself the pain of admitting the truth: I miss David so much, it is almost physically painful. He was my hero. I wanted so much to be like him. I don't... I don't want to be what I've been. The years of frustration over my inability to find him have made me feel like a... a... well, a loser. I've felt weak and inferior, and I've tried to hide it. It all boiled over. I tried to rationalize it, but I was taking out all of my frustration on Miss Flanagan because I resented her for being able to meet him, for having some unique gifts by accident." He sighed, a long, deep, cleansing breath. "Don't be like me, Drisbane. Don't be petty and resentful. Choose your own path and do what you know to be right. Like these boys. Like Carver once did. Let us both strive to be better than we've been."

Steven looked back at him with hurt in his eyes. "All I've ever done is follow your orders."

Benjamin heaved another sigh. "I know, boy. I know. And now I'm ordering you – all three of you – to help me figure out what to do next. I don't know if I trust myself to make the right choices at this point. I need help."

There was a long, awkward pause as all of the men thought about what to say next. Then, without preamble, Eric blurted, "I saw Carver's energy signature in Miss Flanagan's molecular scan yesterday."

John glanced at him, then looked back to Steven and the General, apparently unsurprised. Steven's eyebrows knitted together. Benjamin himself could only ask, "What? How?"

Eric tapped away at his keyboard, and pulled up the image in question. It looked like a bunch of glowing, purple dots in the shape of a person, but Benjamin recognized it as Miss Flanagan's molecular scan. As he watched, a lavender flicker of light crossed over the darker purple dots, and Eric said, "There, see?"

"Show me again, please."

The tech complied. They watched it three more times.

"I'm not sure I understand what this actually means," Benjamin finally said. "It's not something I've ever seen. I didn't think it was possible. Is he actually…. Is he somehow inside of Miss Flanagan?"

"I've been giving it a lot of thought since I observed the phenomenon," Eric said, his mind engaged with the problem at hand enough to make him forget his social anxiety. "We've been taught that Carver could walk through space and time, and visit different worlds and dimensions, even before he invented the Broom. Is that true?"

"Well, yes. Before he incorporated technology, he had to do it the old fashioned way, with spells and rituals and such. The Broom made it so much easier." Benjamin's eyes twinkled as he remembered the joy they had felt after inventing the device.

"If he became lost, and cut off from reality, as we've learned," Eric continued, "he may have begun to drift between worlds without control. Evidence would point to this. We've learned that he would disappear frequently, before his desertion, leaving the room and showing up on the other end of the planet with no knowledge of how he got there."

"True," Benjamin mused sadly. "Very true."

"Well, if he had no control over it, who's to say he didn't start going to places that were not necessarily actual places, but worlds of perception?" Eric concluded, then realized everyone was looking at him, and developed a sudden fascination with his keyboard.

"I'm not sure… I'm not sure I'm following."

"Yeah, it's some trippy shit," John interjected. "He tried to explain it to me and I thought he was having an LSD flashback, but it turns out the kid's never tried any drugs. I think he basically means that every living thing has the capacity to be their own world, as each of us filter everything through our own memories and senses and stuff. So like, the waitress could be a world that Carver might have gotten lost in, or at least visited."

"That's just not possible," Drisbane interjected. "You're combining psychological theories with proven organization methods, and we never covered anything like that in training."

121

John shrugged in response. "It's weird, I'll give you that. But nothing we've done has worked, so maybe we have to consider new ideas."

Benjamin seemed to be staring at nothing, wide eyed and silent, as he considered the possibilities. "If people... if Miss Flanagan, specifically... was seen in that light, as a world...." He trailed off as he tried to frame his thoughts into words. "How... how do we find Dave....Carver.... in her?"

John chortled in response, murmuring, "In her." Once he had pulled himself together, he said, "When I used to play shows with my band, we had good shows and bad shows, like anyone does. When it was bad, it was horrible. It was like the audience was against us. It was the worst feeling in the world, like we were just totally at odds with everything, and nothing was working for us."

"Is there actually going to be a point here?" Drisbane interjected.

"Yes, actually, there is, oh ye of little patience," John answered in a tone that reminded Benjamin of his third grade teacher when her class had been interrupted. "When a show went well, everything just felt so perfect. The audience vibed with us, we vibed with each other, everyone was into it." He paused for a moment. "When we had the waitress here, it wasn't by her choice. We kind of inflicted it on her. She was kind of, if I can refer to my own experience, playing a bad show."

Eric nodded as if this made perfect sense, but both Steven and Benjamin only looked confused. Benjamin finally ventured, "If I'm following you, she needs to play a 'good show'? Is that what you're saying?"

"Well, yeah. Like, instead of trying to force her to let us in to her 'world,' I guess, we need to see if she could just, like, share it. Because if we try to force it, we just get more separate, but if we're all in it together, then we're in it together." John paused for a few beats before saying, "I've studied a lot of science, but the music analogy made more sense to me in this instance."

"I think.... I mean, I think I understand what you're saying," Benjamin stammered. "But I don't really know how to proceed. If I may extend your analogy, what factors were present in a good show versus a bad show?"

"Well," John screwed his face in thought. "I guess part of it was us. The band. Our attitudes going into it, if we were fighting among ourselves – which happened kind of a lot. But it also had to do with external forces like the venue and the audience. There were some people who came to a lot of our shows, and whenever I saw them in the audience, I felt like it would be a good show. This one girl would come a lot, and I'd always play better when she was there, 'cause I kind of had a thing for her, I guess. And there was this dude, this tall dude with dreads, who would always somehow show up for the good shows. Whenever I saw him out there, I knew it would be a great night."

"All of which provides exactly zero help to us at the moment," Drisbane muttered under his breath.

"I guess what I'm saying is, our attitudes toward her might have an effect. We should treat her less like a test subject and more like a person," John explained. "And maybe, I dunno, do we have anything she might want? Maybe she'd be more willing to help us, to let us explore her world, so to speak, if she got something out of it."

Benjamin pondered this for several long seconds before saying, "I think we may have something to offer her, actually. And she may have something to offer us.   She does have some unique abilities, after all, that may actually serve us well."

Steven let out a gasp of air and said, "Seriously? Sure, why not." His tone implied that he was not altogether pleased, but Benjamin had made up his mind.

"We have a plan, then. Eric, John…. Do you think you'd feel better about returning our devices, now?"

Eric tapped the button on the device, and the devices returned to the room.

"Where were they, anyway?" Drisbane asked.

John snickered in response. "They never left. They were just shielded."

Drisbane rolled his eyes.

"Well, then, gentlemen," Benjamin said jovially. "It looks like I'm heading to Woodford to present a lady with a job offer."

Deanna

She opened her eyes and realized she was still sitting on the bench in Woodford. She had no idea whether her meeting with David Carver had actually occurred, or whether it was just a very vivid daydream.

Even if it was real, she wasn't sure if the encounter had done any good. She still had no concrete evidence to present to the men of the organization that she had seen Carver. She had no new information to bargain with. She still wasn't sure where he physically was. Strictly speaking, it didn't really matter whether she had really met with Carver or not.

That left her with few options. She fingered the Broom in her pocket, hoping it would be enough to bargain with. Perhaps the idea of chasing her around the world until the Broom ran out of juice would be daunting enough to cause Larsen to negotiate, at least.

She figured she may as well stay where she was, and wait. Steven and General Larsen were probably already on her trail, and she thought it best to stay out on Main Street, in public. If everything went wrong and they took her away, even if no one else could see them, maybe they would see her vanish. Maybe someone would ask questions. So, she sat on the bench and waited.

As Deanna waited, she thought about what the robed man had said about her being responsible for everything that happened to her. If that was the case, she had better figure out exactly what she wanted rather than letting her uncertainties control her destiny. Obviously, she wanted to deal with Larsen and regain her freedom and safety.

But then what?

Her life had definitely not been going as planned for quite some time now. Actually, when she thought about it, she realized she hadn't had a plan at all; life had just sort of happened to her without any real input from her. She had simply reacted to circumstances. If everything the robed man had said was true – and she truly believed it was – then it was time for her to step up and take charge of her situation.

For one thing, she really had no idea what kind of job she actually wanted. She had only thought as far as finding a job that was tolerable and allowed her to make enough money to pay her bills. She had been so full of self-doubt that she hadn't believed she deserved even that much. Now, however, if she was truly going to be the queen of her world, she needed to figure out what she actually WANTED to do. She knew she wanted to learn; it really didn't matter what the topic was, she simply wanted to learn more about the world and how it worked. She also wanted to help people, somehow, rather than simply mindlessly serving them. She wanted to make a difference in people's lives.

Deanna was deep in thought when Larsen appeared on the bench next to her, causing her to scream slightly and jump to her feet in surprise. As she tried to regain her composure, she grabbed the Broom out of her pocket and brandished it like a weapon. Backing away a few steps, she said, "If you put one hand on me I will push this button and disappear. You can chase me all over the globe if you want, but I don't think either of us want to spend the next few months or even years playing hide-and-seek."

Larsen nodded, smiled, and said, "Quite right. So let's talk."

"I don't know what it is you want from me, but I am not going anywhere with you. I'm quite happy with my brain being just the way it is," she stated firmly.

"I am pleased to hear it, and may I start by saying how sorry I am for my behavior."

Deanna blinked in confusion. She had not been expecting an apology.

"My team has made me realize that I've gone a little off the deep end, as of late," the General continued. "I have been searching for David Carver for about eighteen years now, you see. The idea that you got to see him by sheer accident... well, it drove me a little mad, I'm sorry to say. I realize that now."

"Who is he to you, anyway? Why are you so desperate to find the poor man?"

"I haven't been very forthcoming with information, I suppose," Larsen said, shaking his head slowly. "Again, I apologize. Perhaps you would be more willing to help us if you knew why we were looking for him. David Carver was the founder of our organization."

Deanna's posture relaxed slightly, though she still held the Broom in front of her. "Really? I would not have guessed that."

"Oh, yes. He was a brilliant man. His work is the only reason our organization exists. But he got... sick, I guess you could say. He lost his mind, really," Larsen continued. "Eventually, we lost him entirely."

She nodded to show she understood, but stayed quiet.

"For years, I've been searching for him. I rationalized to myself and the others that we had to bring him in by any means necessary, because he could be a threat." Larsen sighed. "The truth of it is, I miss him. He was my friend, and more than that. He was my hero. I just... I just want him back, and safe. When we found you, and I learned you may have met him, I went a little crazy. I couldn't understand why you got to see him and I can't. I... I think I took my frustration out on you."

"You love him," Deanna murmured thoughtfully.

"I'm not really the kind of man who runs around announcing personal feelings."

"What is it that you want from me, General? It's not as if I have Carver hidden somewhere."

"Not as far as you know, anyway," he said softly. "It's an amazing thing, but traces of his energy signature appeared in your molecular scan yesterday. I realize that means nothing to you, but there's a possibility he is actually – well, that he's actually inside of you, somehow."

She nodded slowly, not knowing what to say.

"You do not seem entirely surprised," Larsen observed.

"I've had an interesting day," she said, her lips twisting into a wry smile. "There's not a lot that would surprise me right now."

"Indeed? Would you care to tell me about it?"

"No."

"Fair enough. May I at least ask, was David involved?"

"Maybe," she said hesitantly. "I'm not being deliberately vague, I'm really just not sure." She took a deep breath to gather her courage, then asked, "Would it be fair to say that he cut himself off from the people in his life, at some point?"

Larsen sat up straighter, his surprise apparent on his face. "Indeed it would. He became more and more isolated, at the end. How do you know that?"

"I... met someone who told me some things," she said vaguely. "That was one of the things he told me. He also told me that you're not necessarily a 'bad guy,' even though you kind of fit into my world as a 'bad guy.'"

He studied her face with apparent fascination. "My, my, you have had an interesting day. I would like to hear more about this meeting, but I understand you may be unwilling to share at this time. So, I will get to the point of my visit. I would like to offer you a job."

Her mouth fell open slightly. "What?"

"I would like to offer you a job. Our training program takes two years, but you will be given a salary even during that time. I don't really know what to make of your gifts and how they came to be, but I'd like to make use of them. With proper training, I'm quite certain you can become a useful operative in some capacity."

A surprised giggle escaped her lips. "I'm not... I'm not going back to that place with you," she said. "I'm not going to be your prisoner again."

"I understand your reservations. Given the special circumstances, and the fact that you've already got a basic working knowledge of the Broom," he waved a hand vaguely at the device she still clutched, "I see no reason you couldn't commute."

For a second, she just stared at him with her mouth hanging open. Then, she began laughing uncontrollably.

"I assure you, I am not joking, Miss Flanagan," Larsen assured her.

"I know... I know... it's just..." she was overtaken by giggles once again, and it took a moment for her to be able to speak. "It's just... this was an awful lot to go through to find a job."

He smiled. "A rather complicated vetting process, I'll admit. But I think you have something to offer us. You can see through our shields, for one thing. And something, somehow, attracted David to you. That says a lot, in my book."

She wiped away tears of mirth and murmured, "It really is as simple as I allow it to be, I suppose."

"I suppose it is," Larsen answered, with a quizzical look.

"Tell me, General Larsen... how do you feel about meditation?"

The question clearly caught him off guard, but he recovered quickly. "I used to meditate. Dave and I would meditate together, sometimes. He stopped before he started getting ill. When he stopped, I stopped." He paused for a moment, remembering. "Why do you ask?"

She ignored his question completely. "How do you feel about the idea of being connected to something larger than ourselves? Or that the universe is working with us, somehow?"

"I...I'm not sure," he stammered. "I definitely feel there is a larger force at work, but it's been a long time since I thought much about it. Again, why do you ask?"

She looked away, gazing down the street at nothing in particular. "Like I said, I've had an interesting day. It's got me thinking about these things."

"I see."

She paused for a long moment. "Why should I trust you? How do I know this 'job offer' isn't just you trying a new tactic to lure me back to that little cell?"

"I suppose... I suppose it will require something of a leap of faith, on your part. But, here," he said, reaching into his pocket and extracting a Wand. "This is for you. I know you don't fully know how to use it just yet, but the mere fact that I would freely give you such a powerful device must be worth something."

She took the device and looked at it, thoughtfully. "I suppose it does mean something. I'm not going anywhere with you today, though. I need to rest, in my own bed, and get my head on straight before I jump back into the rabbit hole, so to speak."

Larsen smiled at her terminology. "Fair enough. Why don't we leave it at this, then – I will be at your apartment at 0800 tomorrow. We will do a brief lesson there on Broom basics, and then head to the compound so you can spend the day with the techs, getting to know our technology."

They looked at each other for a long, quiet moment, sizing each other up. Deanna felt like she was standing at a crossroads, and that her life was about to change a great deal. It made her a little nervous, but she also felt excited. She was going to learn about magic. The possibilities were endless.

She held out her hand to seal the deal. "Then I will see you tomorrow."

He grinned widely and shook her hand. "See you then."

Then he pushed the button on his Broom and vanished, leaving her alone on the street. She shuffled back toward her apartment, suddenly exhausted.

Benjamin

He arrived back at the compound and immediately set to work, getting rid of the cell he had made for Deanna and all traces of it. He visited the techs and told them to come up with a beginners' curriculum for Deanna.

"Word," John said, nonchalantly. "It'll be fun to play teacher for a bit."

Eric only nodded in agreement. Benjamin was pleased by their reaction, nonetheless.

Drisbane, on the other hand, did not fill him with confidence. He went to visit the boy in his quarters, and found him sitting on his bed, looking for all the world like a large, sulking child.

"I don't like it, sir," the boy said by way of greeting. "I don't like any of this. We should take time to consider before making such a sudden decision."

"My boy," Benjamin said as gently as he could, "don't you understand? We may not know exactly what is happening, but Carver's energy signature appeared in her. Don't you realize what that means?"

"They're connected somehow, I know. But we don't know how."

"It's not just that. He could literally be present within her. Bringing her on, educating her, training her – it's the first step in bringing him back." A beatific smile lit up his face. "It's not what we thought it would be, but we've nearly accomplished our mission."

Steven only shrugged, and continued looking sulky. Benjamin left him to it.

He went to his office and made the necessary calls to get the ball rolling for Deanna's training. He spent a few hours outlining the early curriculum she needed to cover before joining the regular class of recruits. He found himself smiling often, and once, a tear slipped down his face, though he only felt joy. He found his internal dialogue, in the quiet moments, said only, "Thank you, thank you, thank you, thank you," again and again. He wasn't sure who or what he was thanking. He just knew he had turned a corner, and was getting Carver back, in some form. He could barely contain his joy.

At the end of the day, he walked out of the building and across the compound, to the shed in which he had kept Carver's motorcycle for so many years. He figured he'd better take it out for a test drive, just in case.

Deanna

She flopped into bed, and fell asleep nearly as soon as her head hit the pillow.

As she slept, she dreamed.

She was back in the great hall full of statues, but the statues were gone. She stood on the pedestal where the headless woman had been, in her previous dream. All around her, people were engaged in all manner of activities. Larsen was riding a motorcycle around the hall, a joyful grin on his face. John, the tech, was playing guitar, while Eric watched and clapped. Steven sat alone, hugging his knees and looking angry.

There were people from Woodford, too. She saw Louis Miller, holding a bottle of vodka and studying it as if he were uncertain whether or not he would open it. Barb, the librarian, sat in a comfortable chair, watching *The Matrix*. The Piano Man sat at a grand piano, playing a sonata she had never before heard. The Friendly Gargoyle walked around, shaking everyone's hands and welcoming them, as if he were the mayor of this strange place.

She watched all of this activity and smiled, until she had the sudden realization that the Rasta Man was not there. In her dream state, this seemed a crushing blow, and she deflated a bit.

"Looking for someone?" a voice behind her said, and she turned. The robed man was immediately behind her.

"Where is he?" she asked. "Where is David Carver?"

"He's finding his way."

"But..."

"Yes?"

"I hoped it was real, before. When I saw him on the sandbar."

"It was as real as you allow it to be. Much like this place."

She sighed, heavily. "I thought... I thought I could bring him home."

You smiled. "He sought me out, for the first time in a long time. It's a start."

"That's...good," she said, uncertainly.

"What is it that bothers you, my lady?"

"I guess... I guess I thought it was time for the happy ending," she said, sadly. "I'd start learning about magic, and he'd go home, and we'd all live happily ever after."

He raised an eyebrow and cocked his head, quizzically. "My lady, why would you wish for any kind of an ending?"

"It's just... so much has happened. I feel like it's time for me to be queen of my world and for everything to be okay."

"And so it is, if you allow it to be," he said, gently placing his hands on her shoulders and turning her around so she could watch the activities of everyone in the hall. "But it's not an ending. There is never really a 'happy ending,' as you say. Only constant beginnings."

Deanna looked around, considering the hall in this new light, as the robed man continued speaking. "Life is constant movement. An ending for one is a beginning for another. It does not just stop, my lady, and rest in some 'happy ending,' unchanging. You are finally learning to rule your world, but what of all of them? For some, the world is changing for the better..."

She saw Larsen ride by on a motorcycle, laughing as he rode.

"For others, lessons need to be learned..."

On the other side of the great hall, Louis cracked open the bottle of vodka and lifted it to his lips, chugging a third of the bottle in a matter of seconds.

"Some worlds are falling apart..."

Steven stood up and punched a wall, hard.

"Others are coming together..."

John finished playing a song and grinned while Eric high fived him.

"And some, you will never fully understand."

The Piano Man stood up with a flourish, taking a bow as some of the people in the hallway broke into applause.

"Your world may fit into some of theirs, or you may pass right by them, in a totally different orbit. However, none of them – or you - will come to a 'happy ending.' Endings, for the most part, are not happy things. But there are always new beginnings."

She looked up at him, confused, and asked, "But what... What do I do now?"

"You wake up."

Her eyes opened, and she realized she was in bed. The robed man's words still danced in her head. "Wake up and be the queen that you are."

She glanced at the clock and realized she had better jump in the shower and get ready for Larsen's arrival. First, though, she had a few minutes for coffee and a cigarette.

Epilogue

David and the robed man walked down the street, hand in hand. They had walked in silence for a long time, and watched the sun come up. David had been content with their silence, but he was beginning to feel he should say something. He searched his brain for the right words.

"Find you again," he finally said.

"Indeed," You agreed. "You did that very well. You must now take your next steps, though."

David looked up at him curiously, wondering what he meant.

"Tell me, David," the robed man continued, "what is the most important thing to you right now?"

David screwed up his face in thought, but he stayed silent. He thought about all that had happened to bring him here. His memories of most of it were just a vague, jumbled blur of images. There was the nice lady who had sat in front of him, saying words that made his brain jiggle. There was a ride on his motorcycle, but it hadn't felt right. He remembered being cold, and walking through crowded places, and climbing mountains, and wading through water, always feeling like something was missing. He had no way to verbalize what had been missing, though; he just remembered this constant, nagging feeling, as he walked, alone, that he was looking for something.

He definitely felt better, now, having found the robed man, even if he wasn't sure exactly why he felt better. However, he still felt like there was something else he should be doing, something that was missing. Perhaps it was something they could do together.

He thought all of this, and he searched his mind again for the right words, for some way to verbalize his feelings. It was hard, though. He had not spoken to anyone, really, for such a long time. He had been alone for so long, he had forgotten most of the words he knew. He wished he knew the word that would explain all of that.

As he tried to think of the word, they turned a corner and he smelled something familiar. Smoke. He looked around for the source of it, barely noticing that he could no longer see the robed man, though he still felt the clasp of his hand.

David saw the source of the smell, then; there was a lady standing in front of a doorway, holding a mug in one hand and a cigarette in the other. He walked toward her, and realized she looked familiar. He knew her. "Nice lady!" he exclaimed, and she looked up, startled.

Unseen by either of them, You smiled and murmured, "It's a start."

Acknowledgements

Writing my first book (which you've presumably just read) has been a lifetime goal. Making it happen while working two jobs, and maintaining my sanity, involved a lot of different kinds of support from various people. I could fill pages with the myriad ways my loved ones have provided support and encouragement, but in the interest of time, I will limit my thanks to these few:

First and foremost, my parents have been amazing in every way. So to my Dad, John Hopton, my stepmom, Margaret Hopton, and my mother, Deirdre Zigarelli, I can't thank you enough for your many words of encouragement, your support, including your donations to my gofundme.com campaign, and most importantly, your belief in me.

To my boss and friend, Adriana Natale Korngold, who allowed me time to write while we were slow at my day job, I thank you deeply. Without that time, I may have never finished.

I'd also like to thank Joe Yerchik, Jeremy Freedman, David Rivera, and Frank V. Scrofani for always being there when I need a friend, and always providing encouragement.

This book was edited by my longtime acquaintance and friend, Jenna Collins, whom I've known since high school. I can't thank you enough for your hard work and kind words, Jenna.

Thank you to all who donated to my gofundme.com campaign to help make this happen, including John Carr, Daniel Mann, Samson Forney, Donna Piscopo, Jonathan Kalafer, Kara Klink Cruz, Jeremy Rogers, Jill Palumbo, and my lovely sister, Jennifer Lee Hopton (and of course, again, my wonderful mother, father, and stepmother).

To all those who provided inspiration here and there, knowingly or unknowingly, for some of the characters and events in this book, I thank you.

Last but not least, I'd like to thank Sara Jane Gasero, who took me to see Neil Gaiman speak at the New York Public Library on Halloween, 2014. Mr. Gaiman has been my favorite author for many years, and while he was signing the Yoshitako Amano prints I had brought with me, I thanked him for years of entertainment and inspiration. He responded, quite seriously, that writing was his only marketable skill. At that time, I had been dealing with writer's block; prior to that, the longest story I had ever written was twelve pages. I had graduated from Rutgers University with a degree in English, then entered the restaurant industry, and was making my living by waiting tables. I hadn't so much as picked up a pen to attempt a story in years.

When he said that, though, I tried to picture a world in which Neil Gaiman had never written his best works because, like me, he was too bogged down with the daily grind of waiting tables and paying bills. It made me sad. I realized that maybe if I just got to work, I'd find that writing could be my only real marketable skill, too. So thank you, Neil Gaiman, for unknowingly giving me the impetus to write my first book, and thank you, Sara Jane, for facilitating that experience.

I actually feel lighter having written my first book, and I promise it will not be my last. You have not seen the last of Woodford, friends.